Praise for the EMILY WINDSNAP novels

'An absolutely enchanting debut – a salty splash of something fresh'   *Amanda Craig*

'. . . enchanting fantasy from a striking new voice'
                    Publishing News

'The wonders of this world are described in detail, from the colours of the mermaid tails to the glowing magic of the coral reef'
                    School Library Journal

'. . . a superb pre-teen read . . . girls will love this . . . since it's not just full of adventure and fantastical whimsy, but also has moving undertones of family and friendship throughout'
                    Waterstones Books Quarterly

'Light-hearted and exciting . . . rich, descriptive passages, unusual in a story for this age group, conjure a vast watery world . . . inhabited by shadowy creatures'   *Books for Keeps*

Emily Windsnap

and the
Castle in the Mist

LIZ KESSLER

Decorations by Natacha Ledwidge

Orion
Children's Books

First published in Great Britain in 2006
by Orion Children's Books
Paperback edition first published in 2007 by Orion Children's Books
This edition published in 2012 by Orion Children's Books
a division of the Orion Publishing Group Ltd
Orion House
5 Upper St Martin's Lane
London WC2H 9EA

An Hachette UK company

3 5 7 9 10 8 6 4

A catalogue record for this book is available
from the British Library.

ISBN 978 1 84255 564 4

Printed in Great Britain by
Clays Ltd, St Ives plc

www.orionbooks.co.uk

This book is dedicated to 'the other SAS',
especially Celia Rees and Lee Weatherly,
without whom Emily might still be lost at sea

Also to my sister, Caroline Kessler,
without whom I would have been pretty lost myself

And if our hands should meet
in another dream, we shall build
another tower in the sky.

From 'The Prophet'
by Khalil Gibran

Prologue

It's midnight, and as light as day.

A full moon shines down on the ocean, making the waves dance as they skirt the edges of the tiny island, lapping on to jagged rocks and stony beaches.

A chariot glides through the sea, tracing a circle around the island. Solid gold and adorned with jewels on every side, the chariot is pulled by dolphins, each decorated with a row of diamonds and pearls along its back and head.

Inside the chariot sits the king of all the oceans: Neptune. Grander than ever, a chain of sparkling jewels around his neck, his gold crown glinting above his white hair, his trident by his side, his green eyes shine in the moonlight as he looks across at the island. He is waiting for his bride to appear from the castle that stands above the rocks, half hidden by mist, its dark windows gleaming in the bright night sky.

'Go around again!' he demands, his voice booming like thunder. His words send ripples bouncing away from the chariot. The dolphins draw another circle around the island.

And then she is there, smiling as she steps towards the water's edge, her eyes meeting his, their gaze so fierce it almost brings the space between them to life. A bridge between their two worlds.

A small flock of starlings approach the water as she does, circling the air above her head like a feathered crown. Twisting her head to smile up at them, she holds out a hand. Instantly, one of the birds breaks off from the circle and flies down towards her open palm. Hovering almost motionless in the air, it drops something from its claw into her palm. A diamond ring. As the woman closes her hand around the ring, the starling rejoins the other birds and they fly away into the night, slinking across the sky like a giant writhing snake.

'I give you this diamond to represent my love, as great as the earth itself, as firm as the ground on which I stand.' The woman flicks back shiny black hair as she reaches out towards the chariot to place a ring on Neptune's finger.

A twist of the trident and a dolphin swims forwards. As it bows down to Neptune, it reveals a pearl ring, perfectly balanced on its brow. Neptune takes the ring. Holding it out in his palm, he speaks softly. 'And with this pearl, I offer you the sea, my world, as boundless and everlasting as my love for you.' He slides the ring on to her finger. 'This is a most enchanted moment. A full moon at midnight, on the spring equinox. This will not happen for another five hundred years. It is almost as rare as our love.'

She smiles up at him, her white dress wet at the bottom where she stands in the sea by his chariot.

Holding his trident in the air, Neptune continues. 'These rings may only ever be worn by two folk in love – one from the sea, one from land – or by a child of such a pair. As long as they are so worn, no one can remove them.'

'No one can even touch them,' the woman says, smiling.

Neptune laughs. 'No one may even touch them,' he says. Then he holds his other hand up, palm facing the woman. She does the same and their arms form an arch, the rings touching as they clasp hands. A hundred stars crackle in the sky above them, bursting into colour like fireworks. 'When the rings touch like this,' Neptune continues, 'they will undo any act born of hatred or anger. Only love shall reign.'

'Only love,' she repeats.

Then he spreads his arms out in front of him. 'At this moment, night and day are equal, and now, so too are earth and sea. For as long as we wear these rings, the symbols of our marriage, there will always be peace and harmony between the two worlds.'

With a final wave of his trident, Neptune holds out a hand to help the woman into the chariot. Hand in hand, they sit close together, her long dress flowing from one side of the chariot, his jewel-encrusted tail lying over the other side.

The dolphins lift the reins and the chariot glides silently off, taking its royal owners away to begin their married life together.

Chapter One

'*E*mily! I won't tell you again.' I opened an eye to see Mum pulling back the curtain across the porthole in my bedroom. Outside, an oval moon hung low in a navy sky. Fourth quarter, I thought automatically. We'd been learning about the moon's cycle at school. 'It's still night,' I complained as I pulled the quilt over my face and snuggled back into my pillow.

'It's half past seven,' Mum replied, perching on the edge of my bed. She folded the quilt back and kissed my forehead. 'Come on, sweet pea,' she said.

'You'll be late for school.' As she got up, she added under her breath, 'Not that you'd miss much if you were. They haven't exactly taught you anything useful at that place so far.'

She'd left the room before I had a chance to reply.

I let out a heavy sigh as I lay in bed, looking up at the ceiling. Mum seemed to be really down lately. That was the third time she'd grumbled about something in the last week. Personally, I couldn't see what there was to complain about. We were living on a beautiful secret island: Mum, Dad and me, all together on an elegant old wooden ship, half sunk in the golden sand and sparkling water that surrounded the whole island. Merfolk and humans together in peace.

I realise that last bit isn't necessarily a requirement in everyone's ideal living situation, but it comes in handy when your mum's a human, your dad's a merman and you're half and half.

I pulled on my swimming costume and joined Mum at the breakfast table. As with everything else in our home, the table lay on a slant, so I held on to my cereal bowl as I ate.

Dad swam up to the trapdoor next to my seat

and pulled himself up to kiss me on the cheek. 'Morning, my little starfish,' he said with a smile. 'Ready for your Ocean Studies test?'

'Test me!' I said.

Dad scratched his head. 'How big can a Giant Japanese Spider Crab grow?'

'Three metres,' I said instantly.

'Very good. Hm. What colour is a banded butterfly fish?'

'Black and silver. Too easy!'

'Too pointless, more like,' Mum said under her breath. What was *wrong* with her?

Dad turned to her with a frown. 'Not again!' he sighed. 'What is the matter with you? Don't you want our daughter to do well at school?'

'I'm sorry,' she said, reaching down for Dad's hand. 'It's just . . . '

'What? What is it? She's learning lots, she's enjoying herself, getting good grades. I couldn't be more proud.' Dad winked at me as he talked. I smiled back.

Dad and I hadn't got on all that well when we first came to Allpoints Island. I mean, we didn't get on badly; it just wasn't easy. I'd spent most of my life without him and we didn't really know what to talk about, or where to start.

I didn't know he existed at all till recently. It was only a few months ago I'd even found out about myself – that I became a mermaid when I went in

7

water. It terrified me to begin with. The first time it happened, I didn't know what was going on. It was in a school swimming lesson, of all places. But then I got used to it, and I'd sneak out to swim in the sea at night. That's how I met my best friend, Shona. She's a mermaid too. A proper full-time one. She helped me find my dad. Best day of my life, that was, when I sneaked into Neptune's prison and saw him for the first time.

I guess it all took a bit of getting used to. But the last few weeks had been brilliant, once all the trouble with the kraken was sorted. That's the most horrific, fearsome sea monster in the world, and I accidentally woke it up! Since then, Dad and I had been out swimming together every day, exploring the golden seabed around Allpoints Island; racing against the multi-coloured fish that filled every stretch of sea round here; playing tag in among the coral. Dad was officially the BEST dad in the world.

'That's just it,' Mum was saying. '*You* couldn't be more proud. And you've every right to feel proud. Yes, Emily's coming on leaps and bounds in . . . ' She paused to reach over to the pile of textbooks I'd brought home the previous day. I *loved* all my schoolbooks. They weren't like any schoolbooks I'd ever had before, that's for sure! For one thing, they were all made from the coolest shiny materials, or woven with seaweed and decorated with shells and pearls. And for another, they were in the swishiest subjects! School had never been such fun.

'. . . in *Seas and Sirens*,' Mum read from the top one. She picked out a couple more books from the pile. 'Or *Sailing and Stargazing*, or *Hair Braiding for Modern Mermaids*. I mean!'

'You mean what?' Dad asked, his voice coming out pinched and tight. 'Why shouldn't she learn about these things? It's her heritage. What exactly don't you like about it, Mary?'

That's when I knew something was really wrong. No one *ever* calls my mum Mary, least of all Dad. Most people call her Mary P. Her middle name's Penelope and Dad's always called her Penny, or his lucky Penny when they're being particularly gooey. Which they hadn't been for a while, now I thought about it. And while I was thinking about it, I guess Mum had a point. I mean, don't get me wrong. I loved all my school subjects. But maybe I did sometimes miss my old school subjects, just a tiny bit. Or just English, perhaps. I used to love writing stories. I even liked spelling tests! That's just because I was good at them.

'What's wrong,' said Mum, 'is that while *you* may be happy for *your* daughter to learn nothing more than how to brush her hair nicely and tell the time by looking at the clouds, *I'd* like *my* daughter to get a proper education.'

'My daughter, your daughter? You make it sound

as if she's two different people,' Dad said. Below the floor I could see the water swishing round as he swirled his tail angrily. It splashed up on to the kitchen floor.

'Yes, well, maybe she is,' Mum snapped, picking up a tea towel and bending down to wipe the floor. Then she glanced up at me and her face softened. 'I mean, of course she's not. She's not two different people at all. It's not Emily's fault.' Mum smiled at me, reaching up to take hold of my hands. I snatched them away, turning my face at the same time so I couldn't see the hurt look in her eyes. That's one thing I absolutely can't stand.

But it wasn't fair. She wasn't being fair. I'd never enjoyed school this much in my life! And OK, so maybe it would be nice to write stories sometimes, but so what if I wasn't learning languages and logarithms or fractions and French? Who said there was any point in those either? Was I ever really going to need to know how much John earns in a week if he gets 4% commission and 3% interest? Surely learning about my surroundings was more important? Knowing which fish were the most dangerous and which were almost friendly. Learning how to look and act like other mermaids, like *proper* mermaids. Even if I did feel a bit silly perching on a rock combing my hair sometimes, at least I was learning how to fit in. Didn't Mum care about those things? Didn't she want me to be happy?

I carried on eating my breakfast.

Mum drew a breath. 'It's just that it's two different worlds,' she said in a quiet voice. 'And I sometimes wonder if they're simply *too* different. I mean, look at my life here. What do I do all day? Sunbathe, comb my hair, maybe go to Synchro Swim a couple of times a week. This isn't a life for me, Jake. I want more than this.'

No one spoke for ages. Mum and Dad stared at each other. I'd just taken a spoonful of cereal and didn't want to chew in case it crunched really loudly, so I sat there with my mouth full of cornflakes and milk, waiting for one of them to say something.

'We'll talk about this later. I need to go out,' Dad said eventually and I swallowed my mouthful. It was too soggy to chew anyway.

Dad left so quickly he didn't even give me a kiss. Not that I was bothered. I mean, I am twelve. I'll be thirteen in a couple of months. It's not as if I need my dad to kiss me goodbye when he goes out!

But. Well, it showed something. Maybe this was all my fault. It was only because of me that they had to try to bring the two worlds together at all.

That and the fact that they loved each other, of course. But maybe they didn't any more. Maybe they'd grown away from each other so much in the twelve years they'd been apart that they didn't love each other at all now, and just had to stay together because of me. And they both hated it, and hated each other, and in the end they'd both end up hating me, too. And now, Mum didn't even like her life any more!

A strange cold feeling started to spread inside me, creeping around my body, seeping into my bones. Only weeks ago, we'd been given a new start on this island. A dream come true. Everything we'd ever wanted. But maybe it wasn't a dream come true at all. Maybe it was going to turn into a nightmare, like so many of my dreams did. Or used to.

Perhaps it was only a matter of time before Mum and Dad decided to abandon ship and not bother being together at all. Then what? Would I have to choose between them? Would either of them even want me if it was all because of me that their marriage had gone wrong? They'd probably fight each other *not* to have me.

I tried to shake the thoughts from my mind as I got ready for school. The Ocean Studies test was this afternoon and I was determined to do well. I'd show Dad that I really could follow in his footsteps, or wash in his wake, as he liked to say.

The thought cheered me up and I even allowed myself to smile as I packed my books. Till another thought chased the smile off my face like a shark chasing off a shoal of unsuspecting barjacks.

The more I did well in my mermaid lessons, the less time I was spending on land with Mum, doing what she liked. The closer I got to Dad, the further away I moved from her. Now I thought about it, I wasn't surprised she was unhappy. I'd been so busy getting to know Dad, I'd hardly done anything with Mum.

Perhaps she was right after all. Perhaps the two worlds were simply too different to coexist. Perhaps my parents weren't meant to be together at all.

I slunk away from the boat, dropping into the water without even saying goodbye, too miserable to speak, too scared to think.

Chapter Two

As I dived down, my thoughts melted away, falling off me as though I was shedding a skin.

My legs felt heavy like concrete, for a moment weighing me down in the water as they stiffened. It didn't bother me, though. I was used to it. In fact, it was the best feeling in the world because I knew what was going to happen next.

My legs joined together, sticking to each other so tightly it was as though someone was taping them together and winding bandages round and round them.

And then my tail formed.

I stretched out like a cat and watched as the bottom half of my costume faded into shiny silver scales, glinting and sparkling and spreading further and further as my tail flickered and swished into life. I would never get bored with that feeling. It was like having been shut up in a box and then taking the lid off and throwing the sides open, and being told you could move wherever you wanted, however you wanted. It was like having the whole world opened up to you.

I hovered in the water, flicking my tail to make sure it had fully formed. It glinted purple and green as I batted away a pair of tiny silver fish swimming along its side. Every toss sent little bubbles dancing up to the surface.

I let myself sigh happily. Nothing could go wrong while I was a mermaid.

I swam along the tops of the coral, glancing down at the underwater forests as I made my way to school.

Bright green bushes waved at me as I sailed over them; rubbery red tubes nodded and bobbed from side to side. A pair of golden seahorses wove their way around long trails of reeds that swayed and dipped in the current, their tails entwined. Gangs of paper-thin fish with bright yellow tails and round-bellied blue fish with black eyes darted purposefully around me. I tried to remember what they were called, just in case it came up in the Ocean Studies test, but they weren't familiar. There was something new to see here every day. I could never tire of Allpoints Island, even if Mum had had enough of the place.

I came to a cluster of rocks at the edge of a tunnel and waited. School was at the other end of the tunnel, in the Emerald Caves. Shona and I had started meeting up here so we could go in together.

A few of the others from my class smiled as they came past me. Most of the class were mermaids. There were a few merboys and two human boys and two girls. I hadn't got to know that many of the others yet, although Shona and I hung around quite a lot with two other mermaids, Althea and Marina. I was the only one who was half and half. The only semi-mer. There was a name for us, even if there were hardly any of us in existence!

I'd got used to being the only one, I suppose, even though I sometimes wished I wasn't. It would just be so cool to have someone else who knew what it felt like to transform like I did.

Well, there was *one* person. The only other one like me I'd ever met, but he hardly counted. For one thing, he was an adult; for another, he was the most untrustworthy, sly person you could ever meet. Mr Beeston. My mum's so-called friend. Who'd turned out to be so much of a friend that he'd spent my whole life spying on us and reporting back to Neptune!

Anyway, that was all history now. At least he wasn't trying to drug us or lie to us any more.

'Emily!' A familiar voice tinkled across to me, sending Mr Beeston far from my mind. Shona!

She swam towards me, clutching her satchel against her side. It was silver and gold and covered in tiny pink shells. Shona always had the prettiest things. She was the kind of mermaid you imagine mermaids to be, all girly and sparkly with shiny long blonde hair. Not like me. I was trying to grow my hair, and it was past my shoulders now, but it still never looked anything like Shona's: sleek and beautiful and, well, mermaid-like, I guess.

'Have you revised?' she asked excitedly as we followed behind a group of younger mermaids with their mums. Holding hands as they swam, they raced ahead to their class, leaving their mums chatting as they glided along behind them.

'Dad tested me this morning,' I replied. 'Think I got them all right but I don't know if I've learned the proper fish.'

'We've got till this afternoon anyway,' Shona said. 'And you know what this morning is, don't you?'

I smiled as I answered her. 'Beauty and Deportment. What else?'

B & D was Shona's favourite lesson. Nothing made her happier than learning a new way to style her hair or get the best shine out of her tail, or swim with perfect elegance. I was more interested in Shipwreck Studies and Siren Stories, but the whole idea of mermaid school was still so new to me that I didn't really mind what we did or what we learned as long as it wasn't long division!

We swam on down the channel. You had to feel your way along the walls as you swam along the first bit. My heart rate always sped up here. The walls, slimy and wet and cold, set off too many memories of what had happened when I'd discovered the kraken in a slimy dark tunnel.

We soon rounded a corner and the tunnel opened up again, growing lighter and filling with colour. I smiled away the memories. I never told Shona how I felt going along that channel. I always wondered if she felt the same way, but it was something we didn't talk about. She'd been with me when I woke the kraken, and was probably as keen as I was to forget about it.

We bumped into Althea and Marina as we reached the fork that led down to our class. Marina swam hurriedly over to us, her long gold tail flicking rapidly from side to side. 'Hey, I overheard Miss Finwave talking to one of the mums on the way in,' she said with a grin. 'And guess what?'

Shona's eyes opened wide, glistening even more than they usually did. 'What?' she replied in the same excited tone as Marina's.

'We're going on a B & D outing!'

'Swishy!'

Althea turned to me. I must have looked puzzled. 'It means we get to go out exploring the reef and the rocks,' she explained.

'What, you mean like when we studied the creeks through the island?'

She shook her head. 'That was a Geography Reef Trip. More scientific. This one will probably have something to do with looking for material to make new hairbrushes, or finding the perfect rocks to sit on the edge of.' Althea pretended to yawn as she spoke.

Marina punched her arm and laughed. 'Come on, you know you love it,' she said.

Althea grinned back at her friend. 'Yeah, I suppose it beats this afternoon's OS test.'

We carried on chatting as we followed the fork that led up to our class. It still took my breath away every time I arrived here. A cave filled with smooth greeny-blue water. Above, shimmering stalactites drooped down from the high ceiling in thin folds like a pterodactyl's wings, or pointed down to the pool like sharp bundles of arrows frozen in mid-flight. All around us, blue and green and purple lights glimmered and winked, dancing on the surface of the deep pool. We swam into the cave, taking our places among the rest of the class.

At the front of the pool, a long scroll hung from the ceiling. In swirly, loopy writing, it always had a message for us when we arrived. Today it read:

Emerald Class: Please remember we have a test this afternoon. This morning, you will not need reeds and scrolls so don't unpack your bags. Leave them somewhere safe for now and please wait for me to arrive

Underneath, it was signed,
Miss R Finwave

'Told you!' said Marina. 'We must be going out first thing.'

A moment later, Miss Finwave arrived and the class hushed instantly. Her blonde hair shone as she swam into the class. It trailed all the way down her back, glistening and perfectly combed. Her tail was sleek, thin and pale pink with tiny gold stars all along it. It hardly twitched when she moved. She always seemed to glide rather than swim.

She was one of the prettiest of the adult mermaids on the island, and one of the youngest. We always took notice of her and tried to do what she said – and tried to stay in her good books. She knew exactly when to praise and when to tell someone off. And she did the praise thing so nicely and the telling off so sharply that we all knew which one we wanted to get more of.

I patted down my hair and tried to sit up straight. We all perched on rocks just under the surface. Shona always looked exactly like the mermaids in textbooks. I tried to copy her, but usually slipped off the edge, or got pins and needles in my tail from sitting awkwardly.

'Excellent, Shona,' Miss Finwave said as she looked round the class. 'Lovely posture as always.' She glanced at me. 'Nice try, Emily. Coming on quite well there.'

I couldn't help the edges of my mouth twitching into a smile. I know that 'nice try' isn't exactly a gold medal, but it was better than a telling off for slouching, which was what one of the boys behind me got.

'Let's have straight backs please, Adam,' she said as she glanced round. A moment later, she nodded. 'Much better.'

Once she was happy that we all looked our best and were paying attention, Miss Finwave folded her arms and surveyed the class. 'Now then, children,' she said. 'This is a very important day. Can anyone guess what is important about today?'

One of the mermaids in my row put her hand up. 'Is it the Ocean Studies test?' she asked.

Miss Finwave smiled gently. 'Good girl, Morag, I'm glad you've remembered the test,' she said. 'But that's not what I'm thinking of. Anyone else?'

Shona raised her hand. 'Is it the Beauty and Deportment outing?' she asked shyly.

Miss Finwave pursed her lips. 'Well, who told you we were doing anything like that?'

Shona blushed, but before she had a chance to say anything, Miss Finwave continued. 'In a roundabout way, it is something to do with that. I shall explain. In fact, I have a very important announcement to make.'

Then she lowered her voice so that she sounded even more authoritative than usual. 'We are extremely privileged at Allpoints Island to receive a visit from our king this week.'

She paused as the class erupted in gasps and whispers. 'All right, that's enough, thank you,' she said firmly. The classroom hushed instantly.

'Now then, I am not at liberty to tell you too many details of this visit. Normally a visit from our king would be preceded by many weeks of preparation. This visit is different. It has been kept secret under Neptune's strict orders. What I can tell you, though, is that a few of the adults in positions of responsibility here at Allpoints have been asked to conduct some extremely important work.' She smiled proudly. 'I am one of those adults,' she said, 'and I have decided to enlist your help. That is why he is visiting us. I just heard the news this morning. Aren't we lucky, children?'

She beamed round at us all. Most of the class stared back at her with wide eyes, excitement shining on their faces. All I could think was, *Not Neptune. Not here. Please no.* I'd only met Neptune twice, and both times it had led to trouble. BIG trouble.

'I thought it would be nice to combine this project with a Beauty and Deportment lesson,' Miss Finwave continued. 'You will, I'm sure, be as delighted and honoured as I am to hear the news of this visit.'

I gulped.

'And I am confident that you will make me proud,' Miss Finwave went on. 'I know you will be as polite and well-behaved as you can be for our most distinguished guest.'

She looked round the class, as though assessing her opinion of us, just to make sure that she was right and could trust us to behave, or daring us to prove her wrong.

Her eyes fell on me. 'I know you won't let me down,' she said sternly. I didn't know if she was talking to the whole class or just me. There was no way I would let anyone down, though. I'd nearly got myself imprisoned the first time I met Neptune, and was nearly crushed to death by a sea monster the second time! I'd melt into the background and keep my mouth shut this time, for sure. He wouldn't even know I was there.

Miss Finwave nodded. 'Listen carefully, all of you, so you understand what to do. For now, all you need to know is that we are looking for jewels.'

'Might have known,' Althea whispered to me. 'Why else would Neptune come here if it wasn't for gold or treasure? What else does he care about?'

'Thank you, girls,' Miss Finwave said with a sharp glance in our direction.

'Sorry, Miss Finwave,' we replied mechanically as half the class turned to stare at us.

'We will split up into small groups and each group will choose a small area of the island and its surroundings, particularly the bays and beaches,' she said. 'You are searching primarily for crystals, gold, that kind of thing. But you will also search for anything you can find with which to adorn yourself in some way. That is where B & D comes in. Remember, children, you are dressing to meet your king!'

I glanced at Shona. She was smiling as though someone had just told her she'd won the lottery. If mermaids have a lottery, which I don't think they do.

'You will use all you have been studying this term in B & D, and combine this with a bit of initiative and a touch of local knowledge. Then you will come back to class and share your findings. There will be a gold starfish for whoever finds the finest jewel, and another for the best decorated child when we return. Remember, use anything you can to enhance your appearance just that little bit, for our guest, for me, for each other and, most importantly, for yourselves. Now, any questions?'

Shona and I decided to go out on our own. We picked North Bay. That's where I lived with Mum and Dad on *Fortuna*. There was something about our bay that seemed to sparkle more than all the others. I was pretty sure anything glittery would wash up there eventually. Also, it had more boats than the other bays. Shona reckoned that made it a good place to find things as there were so many nooks and crannies round the underside of the boats where lost jewels could easily get lodged and stuck. Some of the oldest boats were lived in; most were abandoned and unused.

Millie lived in North Bay too, on our old boat, *King*. Millie is Mum's best friend who came with us to live at Allpoints Island. She used to have a kiosk in Brightport called *Palms on the Pier*. Recently, she'd started doing tarot readings and hypnotism for some of the mer-families because they were so impressed with the way she helped deal with the kraken by hypnotising him. She's a funny one, Millie. Most of the time, she's obviously the world's biggest phoney, but just occasionally she gets something right, and you have to take back everything you've said about her.

I thought it might be an idea to search near her as she always had crystal balls and fancy jewellery herself. Perhaps she'd dropped something over the side that we could use.

Shona swam ahead. She was determined to win the gold starfish for best decorated mermaid. I went along with her, too distracted to concentrate properly. Neptune. In our classroom. Today!

'Fancy Neptune coming to our class!' Shona said, reading my thoughts, as she so often did.

'Yeah, fancy,' I said, without any of her enthusiasm. I thought back to the times I'd met him so far, and how I'd managed to get on his wrong side both times. Not that he was especially known for having much of a right side.

We had an hour before we had to get back to class with our findings. Gliding silently into the bay, I scoured the seabed for anything that could be used as a mermaid accessory. It wasn't the kind of thing I normally bothered with, but I wanted to try to look the part at least, for Miss Finwave, and for Neptune. And Shona was so excited by the whole idea, I didn't want to dampen her enthusiasm.

Mostly the seabed was just pure white sand, soft and powdery. Every now and then, we swam over a rock. We'd dive down and scrabble around it, coming back up with lengths of golden seaweed to wrap round our tails, or shells that had holes worn right through the middle. Great for necklaces if we could just find a thick chain somewhere.

'Come on, let's try this one.' Shona swam ahead towards an old fishing boat that lay wrecked on the seabed.

We swam over the top of it. The front end had been smashed against a huge rocky layer of coral and lay exposed and ruined. Moss and weeds had grown around it over the years. Groups of fish swam in and out of the wreckage that had become part of their habitat. Two black and white harlequins pecked at the rotting wood, covered as it must be by now with the tiniest forms of sea life, perhaps a small breakfast for this pair. A lone parrotfish swam into the hull of the boat. We followed it in.

'Nothing much here,' I said as we looked under the frayed benches and all round the edges of the boat.

'Hey, look at this.' Shona swam into the wheelhouse. Spongy coral had somehow made its way in, filling the little room as though it was a greenhouse. She was pulling at some delicate purple sea fans. 'I could wear them in my hair,' she said, holding one up against her head. It looked like a feathery hat.

'Nice,' I said, tugging at a blue and pink vase sponge. 'Hey, maybe we could use this in class. Miss Finwave could put flowers in it.'

'Swishy idea!' Shona grinned.

Pink jellyfish lined the bottom of the boat. 'Shame they're poisonous,' Shona said as we swam back out into the bay with our findings. 'They would have made nice cushions.'

I laughed. 'Where to next?'

'How about your boat?'

'*Fortuna*?'

Shona nodded happily. 'It's so old I bet all sorts of things have got lodged underneath it over the years.'

'OK. And then *King*,' I insisted. 'I want to see if we can find any of Millie's discarded lucky pebbles!'

'Come on,' Shona said. 'Let's go.'

We swam all round the edges of *Fortuna*. Portholes lined the lower level. Some had glass in them. The biggest one near the front, the one Dad and I used for getting in and out of the boat, didn't. The whole lower floor was half submerged. That was how Mum and Dad managed to live there together.

Green ferns reached up all around the front end

of the boat. It was like an underwater garden, except that we never had to water it!

'Let's take some of these,' Shona said, grabbing at the ferns. She held them against her tail. 'We can wear them as skirts.'

Under the ferns I spotted some silver seaweed, thin and wispy. It was just the thing to help turn our shells into necklaces. I carefully ripped out some strands.

Swimming round the boat, we scavenged under the rocks, trailed along the hull with our fingers, batted fat red fish out of our way, and created sandstorms as we burrowed for treasure, picking up anything colourful that we could carry.

'Come on,' Shona said. 'We've got enough of the B & D stuff. I really want to find some of the jewels. Think how pleased Neptune would be!'

'Hm,' I said. It was hard to imagine Neptune being pleased about *anything*, let alone something I'd done.

'Let's try *King*.' Shona said. Then she stretched out her long tail and swam off. I started to follow her – but something was drawing me away. It was as if I was being pulled in another direction by something attached to me, tugging at me. What was it?

'Shona, let's try over there,' I said without even knowing why. I pointed towards a bunch of rocks nestled among a tiny forest of bushes and reeds.

Spiky black anemones sat along the rocks' edges, lining them like guards. The bushes were grey and dull.

'There won't be anything down there.'

'Please,' I said, my chest aching with the need to look in the rocks. 'Let's just try it.'

Shona sighed. 'Come on, then.'

She scavenged away under the rock with me, dodging the anemones and burrowing into the sand, without knowing why we were looking here any more than I did. A small sandstorm built up around us as we scratched and scrabbled at the seabed, digging out broken shells and pebbles. But nothing more than that.

'How about this?' Shona said, holding up a razorshell. 'It would do for a comb, perhaps, if we just cut away a few ridges.' She turned the shell over in her hands, held it to her hair.

I nodded. 'Yeah,' I said absent-mindedly. But I knew there was something else there. I could feel it shining into me, almost calling me. It reminded me of a game we used to play where someone hides an object and the others have to look for it. Move nearer, you get warmer. Move away and you're cold again. *Warmer, warmer*. I could feel it, close to me. What was it?

'Come on, let's try one more boat,' Shona said. 'We need to be back in class soon.' She started to swim away.

'Wait,' I called.

Shona turned. 'What is it?'

Could I really say what I felt? That I had a burning in my chest that told me I had to stay here, had to find whatever it was that was down here? Look what had happened last time I made Shona help me follow my instincts. We'd ended up disturbing the kraken and threatening the safety of the whole island. No, I couldn't do it.

But I couldn't leave it alone either.

'You go on,' I said. 'I'll just have a bit more of a look here.'

'But there's nothing to see. It's just a bunch of rocks, Em.'

'I know. I just — I just fancy one more scout round.'

Shona flicked her hair back. 'OK, if you're sure. I'll meet you by *King*. Don't be long.'

'Great. See you there,' I said, trying to return her smile. I hurried back to my task as soon as she'd turned away. What was down here? Why was it drawing me in? One way or another, I was determined to find out.

I worked like a dog burrowing down a hole on the trail of a rabbit. I scratched my tail on the coral, my

31

hair was matted and tangled and my nails were filled with sand and broken from tearing at the rocks. But I couldn't stop. Whatever was down here, I needed to find it. I could almost hear it calling me, as though it *wanted* me to find it.

'What are you doing?'

I jerked my head up. Shona!

'I – '

'I've been waiting ages. I thought you were going to meet me at *King*?'

'I was,' I stammered. 'I just – I wanted to – '

'Your nails!' Shona screeched. I instantly curled my hands into fists, but it was too late. Shona swam over to me and uncurled them. 'Miss Finwave's going to hit the waves!'

'Yeah, I know,' I mumbled. I didn't want to talk about my nails! I wanted to get back to my search.

'Come on,' Shona said. 'We're going to be late.' She had some fine wispy pink seaweed draped round her neck. She must have found it by *King*.

'Right,' I said. I didn't make any effort to move.

Shona pursed her lips and pulled her hair to the side. 'Emily, what's going on? You're acting all weird.'

'No, I'm fine,' I said with a lame smile. 'Really. Sorry, come on, let's go.'

I dragged myself away from the hole, pretending I was going back to class with Shona. There was no way I was leaving this, though.

'Hang on a sec,' I said as we passed *Fortuna*. 'I'll just nip in and clean my nails.'

'What?' Shona flicked her tail impatiently.

'Because of Miss Finwave,' I faltered. 'I won't be long. I'll just nip in. I'll be right behind you.'

'I'll wait,' Shona sighed.

'No. You go ahead. I'll catch up. I don't want you to be late.'

She shrugged. 'OK,' she said, and swam away.

As soon as she was out of sight, I went straight back to the rocks. Whatever was down here was pulling me hard, like a fish caught on a piece of bait. As I burrowed deeper and searched, I almost had to hold my hand over my heart to stop it hurting.

And then I saw it.

Turning over one final stone, there it was, glinting at me, throwing light in a multi-coloured arc all around. I gasped out loud.

A ring. A thick gold band with the biggest, brightest diamond I had ever seen in my life. It must have been in an accident, as the band had been dented and bent out of shape. I squeezed it on to my middle finger and examined it. I could tell that it used to be much bigger, but with all the dents, it fit my finger perfectly. Looking down at it, I had the strangest sensation. It was like a tight knot inside me that made me want to scream or cry or laugh, I didn't know which. All of them.

I could have stared at it all day. But I had to get back. Glancing down at my hand every few seconds just to check the ring was still there, I smiled to myself as I swam back to class.

Chapter Three

I joined the rest of the class huddled round a huge flat rock in the centre of the pool where we examined our multi-coloured findings. I'd managed to sneak in while Miss Finwave was looking away, so she didn't notice I'd got back after everyone else.

The rock was covered with a stash that lit up the classroom, splashing a hundred colours all around us. I stared at the collection. Seaweed in bright pinks and greens, shells with the prettiest swirling patterns, sea flowers of every colour, ancient jars filled with sand so bright it was more like glitter.

Bright blue and green and orange crystals, shining white rocks. Neptune was going to be very pleased.

When Miss Finwave noticed me milling at the edge of the pool, she did a double take. Her face turned pale. 'Shooting sharks, Emily!' she said, clasping a hand over her mouth.

'What?'

'Your hair!' she gasped, looking around frantically. 'Quickly, someone get me a comb! Hurry!'

'Here, she can use mine,' Marina said, pulling a razorshell comb out of her rope bag.

'Thank you, Marina,' Miss Finwave said tightly as she proceeded to pull at the tangles in my hair, yanking my head again and again till the comb ran smoothly through.

'That's better,' she said, examining me. 'Now, let's see your contribution.'

My hand was in my pocket. I was about to bring it out to show her the ring, but the strangest thing happened. The ring seemed to be weighing my hand down. I could almost hear it, begging me not to show it to Miss Finwave.

'Shona's already put our things out,' I said, pointing to the sea fans and shells she'd collected while she was with me. I held my breath while I waited for the reply. My hand still firmly in my pocket, I twisted the ring round on my finger so I could feel the diamond against my palm. Then I curled my fingers around it. Safe.

36

Miss Finwave simply nodded. 'Very good. Nice work, you two,' she said quickly before moving on to someone else.

I let my breath out with a sigh. Then I glanced over to see Shona staring at me. 'What's going on?' she whispered.

'Tell you later,' I whispered back. 'I found something!' Now that I'd managed to find out what it was without getting Shona into trouble, I couldn't wait to share it with her!

Shona's eyes went all round and big, but before she had the chance to reply, Miss Finwave had snapped her tail to get everyone's attention.

'Now then, children,' she said. 'Well done. You have created quite a treasure trove in here! Neptune *will* be pleased with you. He'll be with us very shortly and I want each one of you to adorn yourselves with your findings, making yourself as beautiful or as smart and handsome as you can. And the politest class I have ever had, please. Is that understood?'

We replied with a synchronised 'Yes, Miss Finwave,' and then erupted into a scuffle of noise as we shared and compared our findings, bartering and bargaining with each other to get the best combinations of colours, textures and patterns.

I looked around the pool at what we'd managed to do with our appearance. It was incredible how a few bits and pieces from the ocean floor had transformed every one of us. Althea had created extensions from some bright blue seaweed. Next to her jet black hair, they made her look gothic and glamorous. Marina had made a starfish brooch for her bikini top and a belt from oyster shells. Adam had attached a shiny silver crab's husk to some black ship's rope to make a belt that could have been worn by a rock star. Shona and I made bangles and necklaces from the shells we'd picked up, wove the fans into hats, stuck shiny stones in patterns on our tails and surrounded them with swirling patterns made from glittery pink sand. We laid all the jewels we'd found on the rock in the centre of the classroom.

'Not bad, not bad at all,' Miss Finwave said with a satisfied smile as she examined us. 'Very good work. You should all feel as proud as piranhas.'

Just then, a strange thing happened. Strange – but familiar. Horribly familiar. The classroom started to shake. The water in the pool bubbled and frothed. Stalactites shivered and wobbled above us, threatening to crash down and spear any one of us. The last time it had happened, I'd thought it was an earthquake. But it wasn't. At least I knew what it was this time.

'That will be Neptune,' Miss Finwave called

above the noise of water swirling round and round, creating a whirlpool. 'Get to the sides, children. It'll stop in a moment.'

Don't panic. Relax. I tried to breathe smoothly. But my breath came out in sharp spiky puffs.

He wasn't coming to see me. I hadn't done anything wrong, I told myself again and again. I'd make sure I didn't put a scale out of place this time. He wouldn't even know I was there.

We swam to the side of the pool, falling over ourselves and each other, and only just managing to keep our new accessories in place.

And then the water calmed, just as suddenly as it had started. The pool shone brighter than ever, the walls glistened and beamed, the cave was silent as we waited.

The dolphins came first, swimming into the pool in a row as straight as an army's front line. Behind them, Neptune's chariot slid smoothly into view. Gold, grand and adorned with a thousand jewels, it snatched my breath away every time I saw it. I had to shield my eyes from the dazzling light it shone around the cave.

The class fell even more silent. And then there he was. Neptune. In our classroom! Sitting back in his chariot, his golden crown on his head, his trident held high, beard reaching down to his chest, and the deepest frown on his face, Neptune arrived in the cave.

As the chariot came to a halt, the dolphins immediately swam round the back and lined up along the opposite side of the pool from us.

Without speaking, Neptune raised both hands in the air. Holding the trident aloft in one hand, he clicked his fingers twice with the other. A second later, someone else swam into the pool. We couldn't see who it was at first. He had his head down, reverently bowing to Neptune. But as soon as he raised it, I gasped. I'd know that face anywhere: the broken teeth, the odd eyes, the creepy sideways looks.

Mr Beeston.

Neptune nodded to him and he swam to the edge of the chariot. 'Your Majesty,' he said in a deep voice, 'please allow me to attend to your wishes. Whatever it is you need, you know you only have to – '

Neptune banged his trident impatiently on the floor of the chariot. 'Enough!' he bellowed.

Miss Finwave swam forward and bowed her head. 'Your Majesty, it is an honour,' she said simply. 'I have taken your orders very seriously and have set about my work, enlisting the help of the children, as I told you – '

Neptune raised an eyebrow into a wide, white arch.

Miss Finwave went on quickly. 'I have told them nothing of the purpose of your visit. We have merely begun some collections in your honour.'

Neptune sniffed. 'Very well,' he said. Then he clicked a finger and motioned for Mr Beeston to come towards him. Mr Beeston swam forwards again, simpering and drooling like the creep that he was.

'Explain to the children why I am here,' Neptune said to him.

'I – certainly, your Majesty,' Mr Beeston stammered. 'Right away.' Then he pulled on his crooked tie and cleared his throat before swimming towards us. Flicking his tail to propel him higher in the water, he glanced back at the chariot. A brief glower from Neptune was all the encouragement he needed to get started.

'Children,' he began, smiling round at us with his horrible creepy smile. 'As you know, Allpoints Island is a very special and important place. For many reasons. And one of those reasons is the kraken.'

A sound like thunder boomed into the cave. I looked round to see what it was. No one else seemed to have noticed it. They were all looking at Mr Beeston.

There it was again.

That was when I realised it was my heart, beating so loud I could feel it thud in my ears. The kraken. Neptune's sea monster. Had something happened to it? Had it woken again? That was the absolute worst thing he could possibly have come to tell us. Not only would it mean we were all in danger again, but Neptune would remember whose fault it was, who had released it in the first place. I slunk low in the water, trying to hide, trying to make myself invisible. I could feel my face heating up. As it did, the ring seemed to burn in my pocket, almost singeing my fingers which were still folded tightly around the diamond.

'As you all know, the kraken was disturbed recently.' Mr Beeston paused and looked me directly in the eye. Why couldn't I make myself invisible? *Why*?

Then he looked away again, surveying the whole class. 'Well, then. Since that time, I am pleased to say that as the chief kraken keeper, I have ensured no further disturbances have taken place. I have regarded my duties with the utmost vigilance, loyalty and – '

'Beeston!' Neptune growled.

'I'm sorry, your Majesty,' Mr Beeston said, twisting to bow low again. Turning back to the class, he continued. 'However, there are one or two unresolved matters from that sorry period. Not everything is exactly as it should be.'

'GET TO THE POINT!' Neptune exploded, shaking the cave so much that a rock fell from its perch and splashed into the water, spraying us all.

Reddening, Mr Beeston spoke quickly. 'The

kraken held many jewels in its lair. The spoils of many a warship, the cargo of many a cruiser were safely buried and out of danger while it slept. But since the recent troubles, some of these treasures have become dislodged. Items which were buried deep, deep down in the caves under Allpoints Island have emerged or been dispersed.'

At this point, Mr Beeston stopped and closed his eyes. Continuing more quietly, he said, 'Most have been recovered. I have made sure of that. Entrusted with such an important task, I would not have dared fail. However, I – '

'Beeston, that is ENOUGH!' Neptune rose in his chariot. His head towering high above us all, it seemed he was almost as tall as the ceiling. 'I shall continue. Then maybe the children will understand what has happened here. And WHY.'

Pointing at Mr Beeston with his trident, he said, 'Yes, children. What you hear is true. Certain folk have let me down. Those entrusted with the highest of honours have allowed the privilege of my trust to slip through their fins. And as a result, I have lost some of the treasure that is rightly mine. This is not a situation I am prepared to endure.'

He paused, looking round the silent classroom. 'I want it back,' he said eventually, in a voice as quiet and threatening as a rumble of thunder from miles away. 'Every last jewel, every last coin. All of it.'

I felt my hand burning up as though it was on

fire. The ring! It was scorching a hole through my palm.

I tried to lift it out of my pocket, but I couldn't! My hand was jammed fast and wouldn't budge. I bit hard into my cheek to take my mind off the sensation.

Just then, Miss Finwave swam forward. 'Your Majesty,' she said, 'please allow me to show you what we have collected for you.' She motioned to us to clear a path towards the rock in the centre of the pool and waved a hand out towards it. Treasure winked and sparkled from every centimetre of the rock.

'The children have done well, wouldn't you agree?' Miss Finwave said, turning to Neptune.

But he wasn't listening. His eyes feasted greedily on the jewels as he swam all the way round the rock. 'Perfect,' he said, his mouth dribbling slightly, his eyes glinting as much as the jewels. Reaching out with both arms, he swept the multi-coloured gems towards him, clutching them to his chest.

As he glided back to his chariot, his hands crammed with jewels, he turned back to us. 'Well done, children,' he said. 'You've done the island proud. Miss Finwave, excellent thinking. I wonder if anyone else who was set this task has fared so well. I shall visit them all, and reward the most conscientious. Now that I am here to oversee this operation and ensure no one attempts to trick me out of my treasure, I will no longer keep it confidential. You may speak freely of your task. And you may be proud of your work.'

His eyes only leaving the jewels for seconds at a time, Neptune looked round at us all. I'm sure he stared directly at me when he spoke again. 'It will all be returned. Every last item. Do you hear me?'

With one final, terrible stare at all of us, Neptune banged his trident loudly on the floor of his chariot. The row of dolphins returned in a flash, picking up the reins in their mouths. Now he had a chariot full of jewels, he wasn't interested in us.

'Beeston, wrap it up,' he called over his shoulder. 'Return to me if you have any more news on my lost treasure. And not before.'

With that, the dolphins swam into action, whisking Neptune out of the cave.

Once Neptune had left, Mr Beeston seemed to swim higher in the water. When he spoke to us again, his voice contained the old creepy snarl I knew so well, rather than the simpering drool that he adopted whenever Neptune was around.

'You have heard your king,' he said, looking slowly round at us all. 'I do not need to tell you how powerful he is. When he says he wants something to happen, it will happen. It will indeed. And I, my friends,' he raised a hand to smooth down his hair, 'I shall make sure of that. Now that this mission is no longer secret, every single inhabitant of this island will take part in this project, until our king is satisfied. Do you hear me?'

We all nodded. Most of the others looked too nervous to speak. I wasn't nervous, just annoyed. Who did he think he was, telling us what to do like that? He didn't frighten *me*!

Just then, Mr Beeston's eyes fell on me. He looked into my eyes, then glanced towards the pocket at the side of my tail. Did he know? Should I tell him now? I tried to pull my hand out. Again, it felt chained down. I couldn't even move it! What if I could never move my hand again? The panic must have shown in my eyes as Mr Beeston swam closer to me. 'Got something to share, Emily?' he asked, his voice as slimy and ugly as a conger eel.

'No!' I said quickly. What else could I say? *Well, yes, possibly, but it appears to be a magic ring which is digging into my palm holding my hand down so I can't actually show it to you just at this moment?* I don't think so.

He swam closer. 'Are you sure? I hope you know how seriously Neptune would view it if anyone tried to trick him out of anything, even the smallest jewel.'

That was when I lost my nerve.

'I – I found something,' I said.

He moved closer. 'Found something?'

'A – a ring.'

'What kind of ring?' he asked.

I would have shown it to him. I *would* have. I'd have handed it over on the spot if I could. But I couldn't. The ring felt like a claw, gripping my palm, pinning my hand to my pocket. 'A diamond,' I said, feeling warmth flood through me as I thought about the ring. 'A huge diamond. All shiny and sparkly – the most beautiful diamond ring you've ever seen.'

Mr Beeston sniffed. 'There was no such ring in the collection,' he said, starting to swim away from me.

'And it had a thick gold band that was battered and twisted out of shape,' I called to his retreating back.

Mr Beeston stopped and turned. 'Wait a minute!' His face had turned grey. 'Diamond, you say?' he sputtered.

I nodded.

'A huge diamond, a battered gold band?'

I nodded again.

'Battered as though it had been thrown away, discarded?'

'As though it had been through a war!' I said.

Mr Beeston swallowed and wiped a strand of hair from his face. 'I don't believe it,' he said. 'That must be the − 'Then he stopped. 'Where is it?' he hissed quietly, close to my ear.

One last time, I tried to lift my hand. I couldn't do it. What was I going to do? I couldn't say the ring wouldn't let me take my hand out of my pocket! How utterly ridiculous would that sound? No one would believe me, let alone Mr Beeston.

'I lost it,' I said eventually.

'Lost it?' Mr Beeston spluttered. '*Lost* it? You can't have lost it!'

'I dropped it in the sand. Sorry,' I said, turning my face away and praying he wouldn't notice my reddening cheeks. They felt almost as hot as the ring, still burning a hole in my hand.

At that moment, Miss Finwave swam in between us. 'Mr Beeston, in case you hadn't noticed, the children gathered plenty of jewels for Neptune. And he seemed perfectly happy with our work. So I would be very grateful if you could please acknowledge our efforts just a little bit, and leave us to get on with our school day. We have a lot to do.'

'Very well,' Mr Beeston said. With a curt bow to the teacher, he swam to the edge of the pool, towards the tunnel that led out of the cave. Turning back to us once he reached the tunnel's entrance, he added, 'Thank you children,' and smiled.

Then Miss Finwave flicked the end of her tail in a loud snap to get our attention and everyone turned back to face her. Everyone except me. I was still looking at Mr Beeston. He was still looking at me. 'We're not done yet,' he mouthed.

And with that, he flicked his tail and disappeared into the darkness of the tunnel.

I pretended to listen like the rest of the class as Miss Finwave started to talk about the afternoon's test. I pretended I didn't care about Mr Beeston's silly threats, or Neptune's anger, or any of it. Neptune had been here to see us all, not just me. And Mr Beeston hadn't really whispered a threat to me as he left. Not really. I must have misread his lips, or he was talking to someone else. It was just me imagining things again.

I gripped the ring for comfort. At least I had that.

And if it felt as though it glowed and burned on my finger, reaching out for me with a sharpness that almost cut through me – well, surely I was imagining that, too.

Chapter Four

It was hours before I got the chance to speak to Shona. We didn't manage to catch a moment on our own, with everyone crowding round in groups to talk about Neptune's visit all the way through lunch and then having to sit in silence for the Ocean Studies test.

At the end of the day, we swam out through the tunnels with Althea and Marina.

'That was easy!' Marina said as soon as we were out of earshot of the classroom.

'What did you put for number four?' Althea asked.

'Angelfish,' Marina replied quickly.

'Yeah, me too.'

Shona was busy stroking the glittery gold starfish she'd won for best outfit.

'So swish, Neptune coming to *our* school,' Althea murmured.

'I know,' Shona replied dreamily.

'I wonder if he'll get all his treasure back,' Marina added, and the three of them talked about his visit all the way to the end of the tunnel where Shona and I said goodbye to the others.

As soon as they were out of sight, Shona turned to me, her eyes almost popping out with excitement. 'So? What were you trying to tell me this morning?' she asked. 'Was it about the ring? Did you really lose it?'

I glanced around before replying. Some younger mer-children were laughing and playing in the sea on their way home from school. A couple of them had caught a ride home on a dolphin. Others were chasing each other or jumping over waves. The sun beat down on us.

I pulled Shona into a rocky crevice. We swam between the rocks, taking a long route home. Once I was sure there was no one around, I pulled my hand out of my pocket. It slid out easily this time. Twisting the ring round so she could see the diamond, I held my hand out.

'Swirling seahorses!' Shona said, swimming up to

look more closely. 'You had it all along! But why did you say you'd lost it?'

I wondered whether to tell her the truth about the weird feeling I'd been getting from it all day. How crazy would it sound, though?

'You promise not to tell anyone about this?' I said.

Shona looked at me blankly. 'Why? Why the big secret? How come you didn't give it in, Emily?'

I shook my head. 'I couldn't.'

'Didn't want to, you mean?' Shona said. 'Emily, you heard what Mr Beeston said. Neptune will go mad if anyone – '

'I *couldn't,* Shona,' I said more firmly.

She stopped and stared at me. 'Why not? What do you mean?'

I looked up at her from under my eyelids. I could feel my tail quiver as I blushed. 'You'll think I'm mad,' I said.

'Course I won't,' Shona said, laughing. 'I *know* you're mad. Come on, it's me, your best friend. Tell me!'

I smiled, despite my weird feelings about it all. 'OK.' And before I could talk myself out of it, I found myself telling Shona all the things I'd been feeling since I'd been wearing it, and about my hand getting stuck in my pocket while Neptune was at school.

'It was weird when I was looking for it. I had

such a strong feeling, as if it *wanted* me to find it,' I said.

I stopped talking and waited for Shona to speak. This was where she would tell me I'd completely lost it and she didn't want to be my friend any more. Why had I risked her friendship again? Was it too late to take it all back, say I was joking?

I stared down at a skinny seahorse bobbing along the seabed, its bright orange colour standing out against the white sand. A shoal of butter hamlets drifted by, taking no notice of the seahorse or of us.

Finally I looked up at Shona. She was staring into my face. 'You promise you're not making this up?' she asked.

'Course I'm not making it up! Why would I want you to think I'm even barmier than you already do?'

'It must be magic, then,' she said, her eyes shining with delight. 'It's so beautiful,' she added with a touch of envy. 'Can I try it on?'

I laughed. I might have known Shona would want to try it for herself.

I tried to pull it off my finger, but it was stuck. I pulled harder – and a rushing noise flooded into my head. Thundering and rolling. What was it? There was a storm raging out at sea. I could feel it. Waves crashing everywhere, thunder booming into every corner of the sky, lightning cracking the world open. And grief. I wanted to cry. Wanted to break down in floods of tears and cry till I'd filled an ocean. I squeezed my eyes shut, stopped trying to pull the ring off and clasped my hands over my ears.

Instantly, the storm stopped.

'What was *that*?' I asked.

'What?' Shona looked bemused.

'The storms, the sea crashing.'

'I don't know what you mean,' Shona said. 'I didn't feel anything.' She looked at me sideways for a second, then shook her head and examined the ring again. I flicked my tail to stay upright and still as she stared at it. Was she joking with me? How could she not have noticed the storms? 'It's really the swishiest thing I've ever seen,' Shona breathed, still acting as though nothing had happened.

Well, I could do that too! 'I can't get it off,' I said.

'Here, let me try.' Shona reached out and I held my hand open for her. But the second she touched the ring, she catapulted away from me as though she'd been shot out of a cannon, landing in a bunch of mossy seaweed.

I swam over to her and pulled her out. 'You all right?' I asked.

'It burned me!' she shrieked, pointing at the ring. 'Or bit me, or something!'

I yanked at the ring again. 'Don't be silly, it's just – '

'I don't want to try it! You keep it. It's fine.' Shona dusted her tail down, wiping sand and moss from her scales.

I twisted the ring back round on my finger so the diamond could stay hidden against my palm. I felt safer with it that way.

'Come on,' Shona said. 'Let's go back to yours and do our homework.'

She swam off without another word.

I knew as soon as we reached *Fortuna* that something was wrong. The first person I saw was Millie. Not that that was so unusual. She often came round to see Mum.

But she was on her own, sunning herself on the front deck. If sunning herself was the right expression. Millie must be the only person in the world who managed to sunbathe in a long black gown. She never wore anything else. She'd pulled it up to her knees and was stretched out on a blanket, a packet of cards spread out in a star shape next to her.

'Where's Mum?' I called as we approached the boat.

Millie looked over and squinted into the sunlight. Sitting up and pulling her gown back down to her feet, she shuffled the cards into a pile. Shona and I swam up to the side of the boat. 'She had to go out,' Millie said, in the mysterious way that she says everything.

'*Had* to? Why? Where?'

'She just – look, it's not really for me to explain.'

'Fine, I'll ask Dad.'

I swam to the front of the boat and was about to dive down to the porthole when Millie said, 'He's gone out, too.'

I stopped, treading water with my tail. 'They've gone out together?' I asked hopefully, knowing even before she spoke what the answer was going to be.

'No.' She refused to meet my eyes. 'No, they've gone out separately. Your mum asked me to babysit for you. I thought perhaps we could play canasta, or I'll do your tarot cards for you if you like.'

'They've had an argument, haven't they?' I said.

Millie still wouldn't look at me. She started dealing out the cards for a game of patience. 'I really think you need to talk to your parents about it,' she said awkwardly. 'I just don't think it's my place to – '

'It doesn't matter,' I said, cutting her off. 'Come on, Shona, let's go inside.'

We swam silently through the porthole into the downstairs floor of the boat, the part that was fill-ed with water, where Dad lived. I knew exactly what Millie was telling me or, rather, what she wasn't telling me. It was obvious they'd had an argument. They'd been heading in that direction for days.

I'd managed to push the morning's row out of my mind for most of the day, what with everything else that had been going on. But now. Well, that was it. They'd walked out. On each other, or on me, too? Would either of them ever come back? Was it because of me? If they didn't have to argue about how to bring up their daughter, everything would probably be fine between them.

Shona tried to jolly me out of my mood by making silly faces behind the fern curtains and offering to share the bottle of glitter she'd brought home from school. But it was no good. Nothing could lift the heaviness of my mood, or the dark cloud of my thoughts.

Mum and Dad were going to split up, and it was all my fault.

'Emily, are you down there?' Millie called down from the kitchen.

I raced up to the little trapdoor. Maybe she wanted to tell me Mum and Dad had come home! 'Are they back?' I asked.

'I – I'm sorry love,' Millie said. 'I was just thinking I'd make us some tea. I thought you might be hungry.'

I suddenly felt empty, but not with hunger.

'No thanks,' I said sullenly, and slipped back down without waiting for her to reply.

Shona was busy painting swirly patterns on her tail with scale polish. She looked up as I swam back towards her.

And then it happened. The shaking, the rocking, waves rolling over each other; even the boat seemed to be moving. Water sploshed in from the trapdoor above us.

'What's going on?' Shona shouted, smearing the swirly patterns into a smudge down her tail.

'I don't know!' I called back, half of me relieved that at least I wasn't imagining it this time. 'Hold on to the porthole!'

We swam as hard as we could to get to the front end where the large open porthole seemed like the steadiest thing to hold. Gripping its sides, our tails flailing out all over the place, we waited for the shaking to stop.

'Are you all right down there, girls?' Millie's voice warbled from upstairs.

'We're fine!' I yelled back. 'Hold on to the rails, Millie!'

'I am doing!' she replied. 'I'm fine. It'll be all right, don't worry,' she added, her voice wobbling with fear. 'I'll look after you!'

Gripping the sides tightly, our bodies were flung from side to side, our tails hitting the wall as the boat rocked and shook. It was like an underwater rollercoaster ride! Up, down, thwacking us all around, our bodies slapped backwards and forwards in the water so violently I was nearly sick.

And then it stopped. Just like that. The boat stopped rocking. Shona and I looked at each other for a moment as we caught our breath. Just for a second.

In that second, a sharp pain stabbed my hand. The ring! It was gripping into my finger! *Aargh!* I curled my hand into a ball, the diamond tight inside my fist. Catching my breath, I looked up to see a dark shadow fall over the porthole.

Something was outside. Something big. And it was heading towards the boat.

Chapter Five

'**I** might have KNOWN!' The voice boomed into the boat like an explosion.

Surely this couldn't be real. Neptune! He was outside the boat, his chariot gleaming in the sunlight, dolphins surrounding him as he raised his trident. The sea around him bubbled like burning lava.

'Come HERE!' he bellowed.

I looked around, desperately hoping I'd spot who it was that he was addressing. I mean, it couldn't be me. It *couldn't* be. What had I done *this* time?

'Yes,' he growled in a quieter voice that was even

more threatening than a shout. 'You.' He pointed directly at me.

I swam through the porthole that we used as the underwater door, my tail shaking so much I thought it would fall off.

'Alone!' Neptune barked as Shona approached the porthole behind me.

'I'll wait here. You'll be OK,' Shona whispered, sounding as if she believed it about as much as I did.

I wobbled towards Neptune like a jellyfish and waited for him to speak.

But he didn't. He just stared. Stared and stared at me until I wondered if he was going to turn me to stone with his eyes. But he wasn't even looking into my eyes. He was looking at my hand, at the diamond.

'For once, Beeston did well,' he said in a quiet voice. Quiet for Neptune anyway. It still vibrated through the air, splashing water across the sides of his chariot with each word. 'All those years and it was right here,' he murmured, even more quietly, his eyes still fixed on the ring.

My hand burned under his gaze. It felt as though it was on fire, flames scorching through my fingers, screaming along my arm into my body, all through me. I clenched my teeth and waited.

Eventually, Neptune raised his head to look me in the eyes. 'Remove it,' he said simply, holding out his hand.

'I – '

'The ring. Give it to me. NOW!'

As he waited for me to hand over the ring, the sea rocked and ebbed around us. I bobbed about, bouncing up and down on the water while I fumbled and pulled at my finger. My hands shook with terror. I couldn't do it. The ring was completely stuck. My finger swelled and throbbed.

'I – I can't,' I stammered, my words jamming through the thudding in my mouth.

At this, Neptune rose higher in his chariot. As he did, the waves grew sharper, splashing against me, slapping my face, pulling me under. 'Come here,' he said. Swirling my tail round as hard as I could, I propelled myself back up, and swam towards the chariot.

Neptune held his trident in front of me. 'Put your hand out,' he said. I did what he said. Then he reached towards me with the trident and touched the ring.

The result was electric. Literally. I felt as if I'd been struck by lightning. My body zipped into life as though a thousand volts were buzzing through every nerve. Neptune looked as if he felt it too. His beard seemed to have flames flying from it. His tail was shooting sparks out in every direction. A jagged orange light danced and crackled between us, alive and on fire.

Neptune finally pulled the trident away.

Breathless, he paused to gather himself. Then he reached out with his hand. Grabbing my wrist, he pulled at the ring.

'AAARRRGGH!' he screamed, leaping backwards. He shook his hand, blew on it, plunged it into the water. As he did so, the sea raged around us, building into the worst storm I'd ever seen. Clouds darkened, blackening the sky, closing down on us. I was being tossed around everywhere. Even *Fortuna* shook so violently it was starting to break free from the spot in the seabed where it had been deeply stuck for over two hundred years! The boat heeled madly from side to side.

'Damn those vows!' Neptune bellowed. 'They were not meant to prevent *me* from touching the rings! I am the king of all the oceans!'

What did he mean? What vows? Why couldn't he touch the ring?

As if he'd heard me, Neptune snapped his head round to face me. 'That ring has been out of my sight for hundreds of years,' he said. 'And that is exactly where it should have stayed. Never have I thought of it in all those years. Never. Not once did I question its whereabouts.' He laughed sardonically. He wasn't smiling, though. 'Although I should have known the kraken would have found it and protected it. The kraken understands loyalty.'

Neptune looked up to the sky. 'It should have remained hidden, out of sight, buried in the seabed,' he called to the clouds that split apart and cracked in claps of thunder. 'I need it to be buried, along with everything it represents.'

Then he turned to me. 'You have brought back to life what should have remained forever out of mind, forever forgotten,' he said. 'Get out of my sight.'

I didn't need telling twice. I swam as hard as I could towards *Fortuna*.

I could see Millie, gripping the rails with both hands, her legs thrown from side to side on the deck, her black gown whirling out around her. Shona must have still been inside. Ploughing through the water as hard as I could, sinking with every stroke, plummeting down and swirling around before being thrown back above the water and landing again with a splash, eventually I made it to the boat. I gripped a lower railing and tried to steady myself.

'Wait!' Neptune called to me. 'I will not allow this to happen!' A streak of lightning zigzagged across the sky, ripping it in two. The boat swayed again, dragging me under the water and hurling me back up. Gasping for breath, I clung to the porthole as thunder exploded across the sky. It sounded as though someone was beating a bass drum with speakers the size of a planet.

Neptune's face had turned purple. 'You cannot defy me!' he barked. 'I am Neptune, king of all the oceans, and you will NOT take advantage of my laws. Do you hear me?'

I nodded frantically. 'Yes, your Majesty,' I said, my voice shaking. 'I hear you. I – I'm sorry. I didn't mean to steal your possessions. Please, I'll give it back, I'll put it back exactly where I took it from.' I struggled with the ring. Again, it wouldn't budge. My finger felt bruised.

But there was part of me that was glad it wouldn't come off. The ring made me feel – what was it? Comforted. Safe. Important.

'Enough!' Neptune boomed. 'I WILL have it back. And I know how to get it – even if it means invoking a curse that has not been used for many generations.'

'What do you mean?' I asked, gripping the side of the boat as it swayed in the waves that were still crashing all around us. 'I don't understand what I've *done*!'

'It's what your parents did in creating you!' Neptune bellowed. 'And now I shall *un*-create that.'

Neptune paused for a moment and looked away. When his eyes returned to bear down on me, I thought there was a tear in them. Neptune, crying? If I wasn't so terrified, I might almost have laughed. The thought was ridiculous. Neptune didn't cry!

He slowly raised his trident. As he held it above his head, the waves increased, the sky darkened even more, *Fortuna* rocked over on one side. 'YOU!' he boomed over the cacophony of the raging storm. 'You shall no longer be semi-mer. You shall NOT share my world with any other.'

'What do you mean?' I cried. 'I don't understand!'

'THIS is what I mean!' And then he waved his trident above his head, swirling it round and round. As he bellowed his curse at me, the sky began to swirl, too. A dark cone of clouds spun across the horizon, skating towards us, whipping up the sea in its wake, gathering pace, growing in size, and darkening in colour with every second.

'No longer may you be a semi-mer. You will be one or you will be the other.'

'No!' I shrieked. 'Which will I be? Do I have to decide?'

'You do not CHOOSE! You do not have a say. It is *my* choice, your fate. And here is where the curse begins.'

Another wave of the trident; another black cone spinning towards us. I clung more tightly to *Fortuna*, trying as hard as I could to pull myself into the boat.

'You will know the curse is on you as soon as I finish speaking,' said Neptune. 'You will feel its effects begin. In a matter of days, when the moon is full, the curse will be complete. And you shall take your new form.'

My new form?

'In the meantime, while the curse unfolds, you will be neither one nor the other.'

In that moment, I lost the ability to fight back, to argue, even to believe there was anything I could do. There was a tiny split second when everything became calm. The sea, the sky, even the air around me – it just stopped. Stopped dead. Like my thoughts.

'Emily!'

Someone was calling me from the boat. Millie! I'd forgotten about her! She was still on the deck, soaked and bedraggled. Her hair was plastered all over her face, her gown stuck to her like an extra skin. 'Emily! Get inside – quick!' she yelled.

Without thinking, I darted through the porthole – just in time. A second later, Neptune howled, 'I will NOT be cheated. I WILL NOT forgive. I am Neptune, the ruler of all the ocean, and my rule is the law!'

And then it struck us. All I saw was blackness, spinning blackness surrounding us. Then the tornado wrapped itself around the boat, drilling into the sea and sending us spinning.

I couldn't hear Neptune's words any more, but I could still sense his rage, still feel him shouting to the sky as *Fortuna* was raised and hurled in a million directions.

It seemed to last forever. It was like the scariest ride you could ever imagine at a fairground; the fastest, most dangerous waltzer in the world, multiplied by a thousand. I clung to one of the benches that stretched across the lower level of the boat. I tried to scream for Shona but I couldn't even use my voice. My words were whipped away from me as soon as I tried. Was she still there? All I could see was water whirling round and round, a cyclone even within the boat. Side to side, back and forth like a rodeo horse we tipped and spun and clattered around. I tried to scream, but again and again the water snatched away my words, my gasps, even my thoughts.

In the end I just hung on, praying that it would soon stop – and that I would still be alive when it did.

Eventually, the cyclone slowed. It felt as though we'd been in the storm for hours and hours. It was stopping. The boat still rocked and dipped, still turned uncontrollably, but there were calm moments in between. It was in one of these calm moments I finally managed to call for Shona.

'Emily?' Her voice, from somewhere at the opposite end of the boat, was the most welcome sound in the world.

'Shona!' I called again. 'Where are you?'

She emerged from under the table that used to have all Dad's things on it. I shook away the pain that stabbed at my chest when I thought of him.

Shona looked as I've never seen her look in my life, and as I don't think she'd ever want anyone to see her again. The blonde hair that she spent an hour each day brushing was matted and splayed across her face; the glittery patterns she'd been painting on her scales all day had run and splattered into dark smudgy splodges all over her tail. Her face was so white it was almost transparent. She looked like a ghost. A mermaid ghost.

As she swam towards me, I could tell by the expression in her eyes that I probably looked about as bad. At any other time, we would have laughed. I'm sure we would. But laughter seemed as out of reach as every other normal thing in my life. We fell into a hug.

'What happened?' Shona asked in a numb voice.

I shook my head. 'I have no idea. Neptune – he was angry. So angry.'

'I told you what his anger could do, didn't I?' Shona said. 'I told you it could create storms!'

'I thought that was just stories, things you learned in your history lessons. I didn't think we could actually be caught up in one!'

'No,' she said, 'nor did I.' She looked out through the porthole. 'At least it seems to be stopping,' she said hopefully.

Just then, Millie shouted down through a trapdoor. 'Emily, are you all right?' she called, her voice coming out in gulps. 'Oh Emily, please answer me. Are you there?'

I swam over to the trapdoor. 'Millie, I'm fine! And so's Shona.'

'Oh thank the goddess, thank the lord, thank you, thank you!' Millie sobbed. 'Oh if anything had happened to you, I just don't know what I – oh Emily, I'm so sorry.'

'It's not *your* fault!' I said, reaching up to pull myself through the trapdoor. Millie was sitting on the floor shaking, surrounded by the contents of our home, which were scattered around her. Clothes were strewn all over the floor. Drawers were hanging open, glasses and crockery smashed to pieces everywhere. I could hardly bear to look.

I hitched myself up and sat on the floor with her. My tail flapped and wriggled as it started to fade away. Starting from the tip and working all the way up, I felt it turn numb then gradually disappear as my legs re-emerged, tickling like a nerve recovering from a local anaesthetic.

'Come on Millie, it'll be OK,' I said, reaching out to put an arm round her. I've no idea what made me say that. Perhaps I hoped Millie would believe me, and then she could convince me it was true.

Her big shoulders heaved and shook, her head bowed as I tried to comfort her.

As I sat awkwardly patting Millie's shoulders, I waited for my tail to finish transforming. But something wasn't right. It seemed to be taking longer than usual. My legs were fine. A bit numb, a bit tingly, but they looked normal enough. It was my feet. They weren't forming properly. *Come on, what's the matter?* It didn't usually take this long. My toes still seemed to be joined together, kind of webbed.

Webbed? A cold dart of terror stabbed at my ribs. Neptune's words.

The curse had begun.

'Emily, Millie, I think you need to look outside.' I didn't have any time to dwell on my thoughts any longer. Shona had swum over to the trapdoor and was pointing urgently out through a porthole. 'Go up on deck,' she said. 'I'll swim round and meet you.'

I stood up and helped Millie to her feet and we stumbled together out on to the deck, picking our way through the debris that lay everywhere. I tried not to focus on the strange rubbery feeling in my feet as I walked across the deck.

I don't know what I expected to see outside the boat. Don't know if I thought somehow it would all look the same as before, now that the storm had passed, or if there was a part of my brain clinging to the crazy hope that we were somehow still at Allpoints Island.

But if I had thought anything of the sort, I was

in for the biggest disappointment of my life.

I didn't recognise anything. I could hardly *see* anything, for that matter. Just sea. And sky. No island. No other boats, no bay. And not another soul in sight.

There was a stillness in the air as though the world was holding its breath, waiting till it was sure that the storm had really passed.

At first, all I could see was the ocean, deep navy blue, lying still all around us, still as a hundred miles of glass. Just above it, a low mist hovered in a perfect line.

The sun was beginning to set, the sky bruised with clouds, like bunches of deep mauve cotton wool, stealing whatever bits of blue they could find. Wispy grey mists floated higher up, racing the slow heavy gangs below them.

Then the edges of the clouds began to change and brighten, as though someone had taken out a peach-coloured felt-tip pen and was drawing an outline round each one. As though they wanted to make up for the heavy blackness of the storm. Soon, pink and orange seeped into the spaces in between the clouds. The sun forked out through every gap it could find, in bright orange fans. It was like a painting.

A lone seagull sailed across the sky, as though signing off the picture with its own signature.

And then we saw it.

'Look,' Shona whispered. She pointed into the thickest part of the mist. Millie and I peered to follow the line of her finger. Gradually it came into view as we stared, standing out above the mist as though balancing on it.

A castle.

Chapter Six

'Where are we?' I whispered.

No one replied. How could they?

We carried on staring, each thinking our own thoughts, and silently asking our own questions. I didn't ask any more of them out loud. What was the point?

Standing at the very front end of the boat, I slowly turned in a circle, taking in the whole view. Absolutely the same, all around us. Totally, totally still sea. Stiller than I had ever known it, bluer than I had ever seen it, quieter than I had ever heard it.

The boat lay on the slightest tilt, lodged on something. But what? There was no land to be seen, nothing to be seen at all in fact, except the ocean, and the castle, and the mist.

Shona ducked under and swam out of sight. A moment later, she emerged, wiping the hair from her face. 'We're lodged on a sandbank,' she said flatly.

A sandbank. In the middle of the ocean?

Shona shrugged and shook her head in answer to my unasked question.

I squinted at the castle to examine it more closely. It stood, proud and majestic, above the sea: a gothic silhouette against the sunset like a cardboard cut-out. It was a child's picture of a castle, perfectly symmetrical, a turret balanced squarely on each side, a tower in the centre. Two thin arched windows were just visible in each top corner. As I looked, something tugged at me. It felt as though there was a wire between the castle and my chest, pulling at me. I knew in that moment I would have to go there.

The sky was turning red behind it, blacking out everything except its outline and the line of mist wafting around it like cigar smoke. As the mist ebbed and flowed, I noticed the castle seemed to be standing on an island of rocks. Jagged and threatening, they held it high as though carrying it on a platform, a grand stage in the middle of the ocean.

Millie was the first to shake herself out of the

trance we all seemed to be in.

'Right, girls,' she said, dusting herself down and shaking out her gown. 'I'm going to find out where we are.' As soon as she spoke, the feeling about getting to the castle left me, as rapidly as it had come.

Shona looked blankly up at her from the sea, as though Millie had spoken in a foreign language.

'How?' I asked.

Millie gave me a big false smile. Just like the ones Mum gives me when she hasn't got a clue how to sort something out either. 'I'll find a way,' she said. 'We'll have you back with your mum and dad in no time. Just you see.' Then she looked down at Shona and gave her one of the not-real smiles too. 'You too, love. I'll work something out. Don't worry.'

She stepped carefully across the deck and patted the big long sail that lay rolled up along the side. 'Come on, let's see if we can get this up,' she said. 'We could sail back, no problem.'

I stared at her in disbelief. Surely she didn't really believe we could sail *Fortuna*?

But then I thought again. Why not? Perhaps we could! If only we could figure out where we were, maybe we could get it started and sail back to Allpoints Island. I'd managed to sail *King* out to sea when we were back in Brightport. Who couldn't do the same with *Fortuna*? I mean, sure, it was an ancient pirate ship that had been wrecked on the reef two hundred years ago and hadn't been sailed ever since. But we weren't exactly overwhelmed with other options. What harm could it do to try?

Together we pulled and tugged at the ropes and poles, Millie heaving the boom high enough for me to dodge underneath, the sail in my hands. Round and round I went, unwrapping the maroon fabric until it lay across the whole deck.

'Oh,' Millie said, looking down at the torn, fraying, useless sail at our feet.

I looked down at it with her. 'Maybe we could sew it?' I said eventually.

Millie sighed and smiled tightly. 'We'll give it a go, dear,' she said, patting my arm. Neither of us mentioned the fact that the boat was lodged on a sandbank and that the lower half of it was submerged in water. Or the fact that we didn't happen to have the tiniest idea where we were. We needed something to cling to, even if it was an illusion.

'We'll work something out,' Millie said as she turned to go back inside the boat. 'Now I'll just have a cup of Earl Grey and then what say we get started on the clearing up?'

We managed to put everything back where it belonged. Everything that wasn't smashed to smithereens, that is.

The worst bit was when I came across a glass that Dad had given Mum only a couple of weeks ago. He'd painted two hearts on the side with their initials. It was broken right across the middle of the heart, their initials on separate shards of glass at opposite ends of the boat. It wasn't significant, I told myself again and again. It didn't mean anything. I wasn't superstitious.

But I couldn't convince myself at all. It was all I could do to hold back the tears lining up behind my eyes, desperately trying to squeeze out.

It wouldn't have been so bad if I hadn't seen Millie suck in her breath between her teeth and shake her head when she saw it. As soon as she spotted me, she did the smiling thing again. 'It's only a glass, love,' she said. 'We'll get your mum a new one, soon as we get back, eh?'

Then she ruffled my hair and sent me off to the saloon with a brush and pan.

It was pitch black outside by the time we'd finished. I went downstairs to see Shona while Millie made us all some tea. She'd figured out that if we rationed ourselves tightly enough, we could survive for a week on the food we had on the boat. 'Not that we'll be here anything like that long,' she'd said brightly. 'But just so's we know.'

Shona and I talked about what had happened, going over it again and again, trying to make sense of it.

'So he tried to get the ring from you, but he couldn't even touch it?' she asked for the fifth time. 'But Neptune can do anything! Why couldn't he get it back if he wanted it so much?'

'I don't know,' I said, as I'd said each time we came round to this point. 'He said something about his own law stopping him.'

Then I paused. I hadn't mentioned the curse yet. I didn't know how to. If I wasn't going to be a mermaid any longer, that would mean I'd lose Shona as well as everything else that was going to happen. I'd never be able to go out swimming in the sea with her again. I might have a memory drug put on me and never even remember her! My best friend, the best friend I'd ever had.

And there was something else, too. Something so awful I didn't even want to let myself think the words. But they were there, in the centre of everything. My parents. Was I ever going to see them again? If I lost half of what I was, did that mean I would lose one of them as well? The thought was like a kick to my stomach.

'Shona, there's another thing,' I said nervously. 'A really bad thing.'

So I told her about the curse, about how it would take a few days to work, and I wouldn't know which way it would go, but whichever it was, that was where I would stick. I stopped short of telling her it had already started, about how my feet hadn't completely formed when I was on the deck. And how even now, swimming down here as a mermaid, I could feel something was different. Just here and there, a scale missing. Bits of flesh showing through my tail. She didn't need to see that yet, the proof that the curse had already started.

'Fighting fins!' Shona exclaimed when I'd finished. 'That's awful! What are we going to do?'

'That's what I thought you'd help me work out.'

Shona reached out and grabbed my hands. 'I will, Emily,' she promised. 'We'll stop this from happening, OK? As sure as sharks have teeth, I'm not going to lose you. And you're not going to lose your parents either.'

I winced at her words as though she'd lashed me with a piece of wire. Just the thought of it hurt.

'We're going to solve this, all right? You and me, we can do anything, can't we?' Shona looked at me desperately, her eyes begging me to say yes.

I looked at her and squeezed her hands. 'Of course we'll solve it,' I said, lying as much as she was lying to me with her words, and as much as Millie had lied with her smile. 'Course we will.'

I stood on the front deck with Millie. Shona was in the water next to the boat. I rubbed my stomach, trying to ignore the fact that it was rumbling from my rationed dinner of a third of a tin of beans and a piece of toast. A feeling of warmth spread into me from the ring against my body. Everything was going to be OK. I could feel it. The ring was telling me so.

'That's the Plough, and that's Orion's Belt,' Millie said, pointing up at the stars clustered together in tight clumps. I craned my neck to follow the outline she was pointing out. I don't know how she could tell what was what. The longer I stared, the more it just looked like a completely black sky filled with a million billion tiny white dots.

'What's that?' I asked, pointing to a dark shape in the distance. It was coming closer, changing its shape as it slid across the sky. Another cyclone? Please no!

A dark shadow slinking across the skyline, it looked like a giant snake, gathering and bunching up into an arc, then stretching out to form a long black line cutting through the stars. It was heading for the castle. The shape disappeared into the mist, re-emerging above it to swirl around the top of the castle, encircling it, spinning into a spiral, round and round, tighter and tighter, faster and faster, until it faded into nothing.

We stared into the black night. The shape didn't come back.

'I have no idea,' Millie said eventually. 'And I'm not one for superstition, as you know, but I'll bet it's portentous. Let me have a think.'

'What about the stars though?' Shona said. 'There are constellations that can help us work out where we are, I'm sure of it. I just can't remember what they're called. Or what they look like.'

Which was a big help.

'I've got it!' Millie said, her eyes brightening. 'I've had a great idea.' She headed back inside the boat and beckoned me to follow.

For a moment, for one silly, ridiculous, heart-stopping moment, I actually thought she'd come up with a plan to get us out of this. I let myself hope. Until she said, 'I'll do our tarot cards.'

I followed Millie into the kitchen. 'You clear a spot for us in the saloon and I'll lay out the cards,' she said.

Shona swam up to the trapdoor as I pushed a couple of chairs to the side. She poked her head through and I sat on the floor by the trapdoor to join her. Then Millie came in with the cards and we watched intently as she shuffled, spread the cards in a six-pointed star and slowly turned them over, one by one. She didn't speak, didn't explain anything. When they were all face up, she sat looking at them for ages, nodding slowly.

'What do they say?' Shona asked.

'Do they say anything about my mum and dad?' I asked.

'Or mine,' Shona added quietly. That was the first time I had really thought about her parents. She'd been taken away from them, too. They wouldn't have a clue what had happened to her. They hadn't seen her since she went to school that morning. I'd been so selfishly wrapped up in my own problems, I hadn't thought about Shona's.

Would anyone tell them anything back at Allpoints Island? What would happen when Mum and Dad came home – assuming they ever did – and found that *Fortuna* wasn't even there? Would they come after us? Would they know where to look? They'd find out, wouldn't they? But what if they didn't? Suppose they didn't come home at all! Suppose they'd had such a row they'd split up and both forgotten all about me!

No! I couldn't let myself think like that. I couldn't! Surely they'd do something. They'd get together with Shona's parents and send out a search party or something.

They'll find us. They'll find us. They'll find us. I repeated the phrase over and over and over like a mantra. *Please let me believe it*, I added.

The cards didn't tell us anything. Anything beyond what they normally said when Millie read anyone's tarot cards. We had a long journey ahead and the outcome was uncertain. A tall skinny stranger with jet black hair would help guide us, the truth would elude us and all would be well in the end. Blah. Why I ever put faith in Millie's card reading I don't know. It was about as useful as trying to tell the time from examining your freckles.

'Look, let's all try and get a bit of sleep,' she said, shuffling the cards away when it was clear they hadn't impressed any of us, or helped us find an answer to any of the questions we weren't asking out loud. 'Things are bound to look better in the morning, once we've had a few hours' nap – and perhaps a cup or two of Earl Grey.'

I stifled a laugh. Admittedly, a slightly hysterical one. It was really rather hard to see how things were going to look better. But she had a point about the sleep thing. I was exhausted.

'Shona, you take Jake's room,' Millie said. 'You'll be all right down there, won't you?'

Shona bit her lip and nodded.

'I'll join you if you like,' I said softly.

'No, you're OK. I'll be fine.'

'I'll be just above you. Knock if you need me.'

Shona smiled, although her eyes stayed misty and sad.

'It'll look better in the morning,' I said, repeating Millie's lie. It kind of helped to keep saying these things out loud. If we did it often enough, perhaps they'd come true.

'Night night, you two,' Millie said. 'I'm going to get some shut-eye myself now. Although goddess only knows how I'll sleep without my agnus castus tablets.'

We each withdrew to our own rooms, our own thoughts and our own fears.

The moon rose as I lay on my bed. I watched it climb past the porthole. A fat wonky shape like a slightly deflated ball, it shone down on me, right at me as though it was personal. Just me and the moon, staring each other out.

The black sky, endless behind it, filled slowly with clouds, some huge and unmoving like snow-clad hills, others grey and broken up like crazy paving. Lighter wispy clouds sailed slowly in front of them all. And the moon stood firm, almost whole, like a circle drawn freehand by a child. Not quite perfect but not far off.

Please let this be a dream, I whispered, twisting the ring round and round on my finger, talking to it as though it could hear my thoughts and turn them into reality. Was it a friend or enemy? What was its hold over Neptune – and over me? I couldn't tell. All I had was the knowledge that it was caught up in this whole nightmare with us – and the tiny feeling that it might help us find our way out of it, too.

Please let me be back at Allpoints Island in the morning, I prayed. Please let me hear Mum and Dad arguing in the kitchen as soon as I wake up. Please.

Next time I looked, the clouds had all moved on. The stars were no longer visible either. Just the moon remained, bright and proud. *See?* it seemed to snigger at me. *I win.*

There was a split second when I woke up when everything felt normal. Any second now, Mum would call me to get up and I'd have to drag myself out of bed. She hadn't called yet, though. Still half asleep, I stretched and turned over in my warm bed. I was about to go back to my dreams – and then I remembered.

I sat bolt upright, then jumped out of bed and ran to the porthole. Let me see Allpoints Island. Let us be back there.

I was greeted by the sight of mauve sea stretching out forever, everywhere I looked. Baby blue sky. And the white line of mist hovering in the middle, dividing the two worlds.

'Emily, are you up?' Shona's voice called quietly from below.

I ran to the trapdoor and dropped myself down to join her. As soon as my legs touched the water, I felt them change. *Please work properly this time,* I said silently to myself, and I held my breath as I felt my tail form. Closing my eyes, I focused for a moment on the feeling, willing it to work completely. But it didn't. In fact, it was even worse. Patches of scales were missing, the shine of my sparkling tail seemed duller, my tail moved more stiffly.

I swallowed my feelings down and hoped Shona wouldn't notice. I still didn't want to admit it out loud. I wasn't a mermaid half the time any more. Now I wasn't even a proper mermaid at all.

'Look.' Shona pulled me over to the large porthole door. We swam out through it, round the huge sandbank under the boat, and up to the surface where we trod water by the side of the boat. Directly ahead of us, hovering on the line of mist as though it was floating, the castle stood bold and gleaming in the sunlight. 'I think we should go to it,' Shona said, echoing my thoughts from yesterday.

'On the boat? How? You saw the sails.'

Shona was shaking her head. 'No, I meant just

you and me. We could swim there. It doesn't look far.'

It was still early. I could tell by how low the sun was in the sky. In fact, now I looked, I could still see the moon, hanging on like the last guest at a party, reluctant to leave but fading and tired. Millie would still be in bed. She always slept late. We could get there. As soon as the thought came into my mind, my hand grew hot. The ring – it was telling me something, I was sure of it!

It was telling us to go.

'Come on,' I said, feeling hopeful for the first time since we'd landed here. 'Let's do it.'

Chapter Seven

'How long have we been swimming?' I asked, panting to catch up with Shona. Surely she was swimming faster than usual! I could hardly keep alongside her.

'Not sure. Maybe twenty minutes, half an hour tops.'

I stopped where we were and flicked my tail round in fast circles to tread water. 'Look,' I said, pointing to the castle. It seemed to be looking back at me, willing me to approach it. Pulling me along. But there was a problem. A big problem.

Shona looked across at the castle. 'What?'

'It's no nearer. It looks just as far away as it was from the boat.'

'Don't be daft,' Shona said with a laugh. 'It's just . . . ' Then she glanced back to see where we'd come from. *Fortuna* was a dot in the distance. She turned back towards the castle. 'But that's . . . but it's not possible.'

'It's like a rainbow,' I said. 'The nearer you get to it, the further away it seems.'

'But how?' Shona's voice broke into a whine. Her eyes moistened as her bottom lip began to tremble. I almost expected her to howl, 'I want my mummy!' And why shouldn't she? That was certainly what I wanted to do. I felt like a burst balloon.

'Come on,' I said flatly. 'Let's go back to the boat. Maybe Millie will have some idea what's going on. You know she thinks more clearly in the mornings once she's had a cup of tea.'

'Or ten,' Shona added with a hint of a smile.

I smiled back. 'We'll figure it out,' I said. 'Don't worry.'

As we swam back, I didn't tell her how stiff my tail was getting, how it was starting to feel as if I was dragging a lead weight behind me. I pretended I wanted to go more slowly to take in the view: the sea, calm and smooth as we cut through it, the mist lying low and still on its surface.

Eventually, we got back to the boat and swam in through the porthole. Almost as soon as we did, Millie's voice warbled down to us. 'Emily? Shona? Is that you?' she called, an edge of panic in her voice.

'Hi! We're here!' I called back.

'Oh, thank heavens,' Millie breathed, her face appearing at the trapdoor as she leaned over it to look down at us. 'Where have you been?'

'We just went out for a quick swim,' I said.

'Emily.' Millie's tone had turned serious. Her voice a low rumble, she said sternly, 'You must never, ever go out without telling me again. I am responsible for you. I will never forgive myself if anything happened to you. Do you hear me?'

'I'm sorry,' I said. 'We were just – '

'It doesn't matter now.' Millie waved the rest of my sentence away. Just then, I heard a cough from somewhere behind her.

'Who's that?' I blurted out. My heart lifted. Millie had been kidding me! Mum and Dad were here! They were waiting for the right moment and were going to appear any second, big smiles, and tell me this had all been a joke, or a mistake or –

'There's someone to see you,' Millie said in a voice as flat and lifeless as a dead eel. And then, cutting my hopes like the sharpest knife, a face appeared next to hers.

Mr Beeston.

'Hello girls,' he said, squinting down at me and Shona.

'What are you doing here?' I asked through a tight throat. 'How did you find us? Where are my parents?'

'Now, now,' Mr Beeston said with a crooked half-smile. How could he smile? Didn't he understand anything that was going on? Or was I mistaking him for someone who cared? 'One thing at a time. You calm yourself down and then meet me on the front deck.' He nodded at Shona. 'And you, child,' he said. 'You'll all need to hear what I have to say.' He pulled back a sleeve of his old nylon suit to glance at his watch. 'Let's say ten minutes.' And then he'd gone.

'I'll be with you,' Millie said softly. 'I'm not going to leave your side till we've got this sorted, right?'

I nodded. My throat felt too thick and too dry to speak.

Mr Beeston was waiting on the front deck, sitting on a bench looking round at the horizon.

'Now then,' he said as Millie and I sat on the opposite bench. Shona perched on the edge of the deck, her tail draped loosely over the side, flicking the water with tiny splashes. *How much longer will I be able to do that, too?* I glanced at my hands. The skin reached up along my fingers, joining them together, lodging the ring even more tightly in place. What was happening to my body? It was just as Neptune had said. Until the curse was complete, I wouldn't be one thing or another. What did that make me? A nothing?

I couldn't bear to see the evidence, so I stuffed my hands in my jeans pockets and waited for Mr Beeston to explain what was going on.

He cleared his throat. 'Now then,' he said again. 'You are probably wondering why I'm here.'

D'you THINK?

I bit my lip. It was never a good idea to interrupt Mr Beeston. It only took another half an hour for him to get going again. He wasn't a big fan of sarcasm either – or of cheek. Or of me. So I kept my mouth shut and counted to ten.

'As you know, I was entrusted by Neptune with a most important job. And as you also know, there had been a certain amount of disturbance which I was in the process of endeavouring to correct. In fact, even as I speak, some of the folk at Allpoints Island are gathering the final few items of lost treasure. The project has been very successful, largely thanks to your resourceful teacher. All of which helps make Neptune happy. However, as we *all* know . . . ' At this point, he looked round at the three of us with one of his crooked smiles, trying to include us as though we were all in this together. How could we be when he was the only one who had any idea what was going on?

Again, I stopped myself from saying anything. I counted to twenty this time.

'As we all know,' he repeated, 'the situation has changed somewhat. Since events took the turn they did, Neptune's attention has wandered from his initial intentions. And so we have found ourselves in this situation.'

He folded his hands in his lap.

'What situation?' Millie asked. 'I haven't got the slightest idea what you are talking about. Now are you going to explain what in the cosmos is going on here or am I going to have to – '

'Calm down, calm down.' Mr Beeston waved a hand at her. 'I am coming to it.'

Then he fixed his eyes on the ring. 'Emily here has found something we never even realised was there, something that Neptune wants back, and perhaps if I tell you a little bit about it, you will understand why. Then maybe we can work together to solve the problem and all will be well.'

'All will be well?' I exploded. I couldn't stop myself this time. There weren't enough numbers to count to that would halt my rage. 'All well? We're lost out in the middle of the ocean, with nothing but sea and mist and a spooky castle that doesn't even seem to exist. Shona's parents haven't seen her since yesterday morning. *My* parents have fallen out and probably never want to see each other or me again – '

'Come on Emily, you know that's not true,' Millie interrupted me.

I ignored her. 'And to top it all, Neptune's done *this*!' I pulled my hands from my pockets and held them out in front of me. The skin had reached even further up my fingers. They were joined at least a third of the way up, lodging the ring so tightly on my finger it hurt.

'Emily!' Shona gasped, edging forward to look more closely at my hands. 'What's that?' She looked disgusted. I knew she would.

'I didn't want to tell you,' I said. 'I didn't know if you'd still want to be my friend if you knew.'

'Knew what?'

'The curse. It's already started,' I said. 'I'm not a proper mermaid any more, or a proper girl. I'm nothing.'

I felt a couple of tears roll down my cheeks, salty drips running into my mouth. Millie was gazing at the ring. 'What in the name of the goddess is that?' she breathed. 'And where did you get it?'

Mr Beeston pulled at his tie. 'Millicent, if you will allow me to explain.'

Millie waved a hand at him. 'Go on. Whatever you've got to say can't make things any worse, I suppose. Just say what you've come to say and get on with it. And then maybe you can go away again and leave us to work out what to do next.'

'I shall indeed say what I have come to say,' he said, in that annoying I'm-so-much-more-important-than-you voice of his. 'If you will let me.'

Mr Beeston pulled on his tie and flattened down his hair again, and eventually said, 'You need to understand the importance of what you have here, Emily.'

'What I have where?' I asked. As if I didn't know.

Mr Beeston pointed at my hand. 'There,' he said simply. 'You see, this ring has lain out of sight, hidden and protected by the kraken, for many years. For generations.'

'Why is it so important if it's been buried all that time?' Shona asked. 'Why was it buried at all if it's that important?'

'It wasn't. It was discarded.'

'Discarded?' Millie burst out. 'Who by?'

'By Neptune.'

For a moment, we all fell silent. Then in an even voice, Millie quietly said, 'Charles, we would appreciate it if you could stop talking in riddles and please explain what is going *on* here.'

'I shall tell you everything!' Mr Beeston blustered. Then he paused for ages, clasping his hands together and looking out to the still sea that lay waiting silently like the rest of us. 'Many many years ago, Neptune was in love,' he began. 'As you know, he loves easily, and has many wives, but none like this one. None like Aurora.'

'Aurora!' Shona interrupted. 'But I've heard of her! She's the human. The one who broke his heart. The one who turned him against intermarriage and everything. We did it last year in history!'

Mr Beeston nodded. 'Exactly.'

I couldn't help holding my breath while I waited for him to continue.

'Aurora was the only wife Neptune truly loved with all his heart. When they married, they had rings made to symbolise their love. One contained a diamond, to represent land. The other held a pearl, to represent the sea. On the day of their marriage, they exchanged these rings. Aurora gave the diamond ring to Neptune. He gave her the pearl.'

I touched the diamond as he spoke. I was wearing a ring that was given to Neptune on his wedding day? Given to him by a wife who left him and broke his heart? No wonder he had gone into such a rage! But how was I to know? It wasn't my fault!

No. It wasn't your fault, a voice seemed to echo. Not even in words; it was just a feeling. A feeling of comfort and reassurance – and it was coming from the ring. Twisting it round to hold the diamond against my palm, I curled my fingers around it, my heartbeat settling as I did so.

'On the day she broke his heart, Neptune took her ring from her and buried it.'

'Where?' I asked.

'That I cannot tell you,' Mr Beeston said. 'That information is not something you need to have.'

He spoke so haughtily I knew it wasn't worth asking again. It would only give him the chance to refuse me again, and make himself feel even more self-important than he already did.

But I couldn't help wondering about it. There was another ring similar to mine, buried out in the sea somewhere. A ring Mr Beeston didn't want me to ask about – which in itself meant it was probably important!

'What about his own ring, the diamond one?' Millie asked.

'In his rage, Neptune hurled it with all his might across the oceans. This is the first time it has been seen since that day. No one knows when the kraken found it. All we know is that it did, and it kept it safe and hidden with the many other jewels at Allpoints Island.'

'And when the kraken woke, the ring was disturbed with the rest of the jewels?' Shona asked.

'Exactly.'

'And now he wants it back.' I swallowed. 'But it

won't come off me.'

'Why not?' Millie asked.

Mr Beeston looked down, flattening his jacket and picking off an imaginary speck of dust. His suit was wonky as usual, a button missing on one side, a hole overlooked on the other. 'The rings can only be worn by certain folk. Either by a couple where one is from the land and the other is from the sea, or a child of such a couple. It was in the wedding vows between Neptune and Aurora, and the rings were infused with this power. Worn by a semi-mer, this ring cannot be removed.'

'Sharks!' Shona breathed.

'So how did he remove their rings in the first place?' Millie asked.

Mr Beeston sniffed. 'The love was dead. The connection was broken.'

'That's why he cursed me,' I said quietly. 'So he can remove the ring.'

'Correct. When the moon is full, the spell will be complete. You will no longer be a semi-mer. You will not be able to touch the ring – and it will not be able to touch you. It will fall from you as you would jump from a fire.'

'And Neptune can have it back,' Shona said.

'He wants it hidden again, along with his memories and his long-buried grief. He cannot exist like this, and if Neptune can't live, none of us can. You yourselves have felt the effect of his current state. It will only get worse. That is what we would all have to look forward to if the ring is not buried again. Just more of that and nothing else, for the whole mer-world.' He turned to me. 'Is that what you want, Emily? Is it not an honour to make a sacrifice like this for your king?'

I couldn't speak.

'So why are you here?' Millie asked coldly. 'Has he sent you to do his dirty work?'

'Dirty work?' Mr Beeston spat. 'Dirty work? I consider it the highest of honours to be called to duty by my king, to be graciously offered the opportunity to make amends for my earlier failure.' He pulled himself up straighter in his seat.

'Like I said, do his dirty work,' Millie said under her breath.

'I am responsible for this ring, and I will ensure it is returned to Neptune. Make no mistake, that is what I will do,' Mr Beeston concluded.

'How did you find us?' I asked numbly.

'The ways of our king are immeasurable. He made it possible for me to be here. That is all I need to know. It is not for you – or me – to question his methods beyond this.'

'That means he's got no idea,' Millie said. I smiled, despite everything.

'I have to go soon,' Mr Beeston said, ignoring her as he glanced around at the endless ocean, as though waiting for his signal to leave. The ocean responded in the same way as it did to everything else – with silence and stillness. Then he turned to me. 'But Emily, I shall not be far away. I shall be back very soon.'

'How will you get back? Can't you let us go with you?' I asked, knowing it was pointless as soon as I'd uttered the words.

'I'm sorry. I have to do as bidden by my king. You will stay here for now.'

'How far are we from Allpoints Island?' I asked, edging closer to the questions I really wanted to ask.

'Many hundreds of miles.'

I nodded. Another kick, this time in my chest. Finally I said, 'And what about Mum and Dad? Where are they? Do they know what's happened? Are they going to come after us? Will they find us, too?' The questions ran out in a rush. My heart banged in my ears like thunder while I waited for his reply.

Mr Beeston puffed out his chest. 'Your parents do not know your whereabouts,' he said, in that oh-I'm-*so*-important voice again.

'Where are they?' I asked, holding back my anger.

'Your mother is staying on the old boat.'

'On *King*?' Millie asked.

He nodded.

'Does she know what's happened?' I asked.

'She knows only that you have been called upon to assist Neptune in a grave matter.'

'Has she looked for me?' My throat was full of knives.

Mr Beeston lowered his head. 'She has, yes. We've told her you're not at the island. The other islanders will look after her, and I am close at hand to support both your mother and Shona's parents.'

'And Dad?' I asked. 'Where's he staying?'

Mr Beeston at least had the decency to look slightly uncomfortable this time as he looked at me. What did he see in my face? A reminder that every word he uttered was crashing into my world like a sledgehammer? 'I'm afraid they have been separated,' he mumbled. 'He is staying with Archieval for now.'

Archie was another of Neptune's helpers, and my dad's friend. At least they both had people around them who cared, not just slimeballs like Mr Beeston, I told myself, desperately grasping at anything that might provide a grain of comfort.

'Why have they been separated?' I asked.

'Neptune has decided to go back to the old ways.'

'What old ways?' Shona asked.

'He's banned intermarriage again. For good, this time. He says he has had enough of the trouble it causes.' Mr Beeston looked me in the eyes.

'Your parents will not be together again,' he said drily.

And that was it. The end of my world. With those simple words. Game over. My insides turned cold and hardened. At that moment, I believe I could have broken into a thousand pieces.

In a matter of days, I would no longer be a mermaid. Or I'd be a mermaid and would never again be able to live on land. And my parents would never see each other again. With a feeling of utter horror, I realised what this meant: I couldn't have both parents. I would have to say goodbye to one of them forever.

'No!' I begged. I pulled on Mr Beeston's arm. 'Please, no!' Tears hurtled down my face. '*Please,*' I begged. 'You have to make Neptune change his mind. You have to do something. Please!'

'There is nothing that will change his mind,' Mr Beeston said, his voice steady and cold. 'Neptune's word is law. Your parents will come together one last time when Neptune brings them to you. Under the full moon, when the curse is complete, you will have a chance to say goodbye to one parent. You will go home with the other.'

'No!' I fell to my knees in front of him. I hated myself for begging Mr Beeston, of all people. But it couldn't happen. It *couldn't* happen. It couldn't.

But as Mr Beeston shook me away and dived off the side of the boat, disappearing deep down into

the sea, I knew the truth. It was going to happen.
It really, really was. And there wasn't a single thing
I could do to stop it.

Chapter Eight

'Right, that settles it,' Millie said, blowing on a cup of tea. 'I'm not letting you out of my sight. If Neptune can send Mr Beeston here from nowhere, who knows what might happen if you went out there?' She cocked her head to point out at the endless ocean. 'You could be kidnapped and taken away forever.' She shuddered. Then she reached out to pat my knee. 'You're my responsibility now, lovey,' she said gently. 'And I'm going to look after you.'

True to her word, she didn't leave us alone after

that. Which meant Shona and I didn't get another chance to try to swim to the castle, or even talk about it.

The day passed in a blur of Earl Grey, beans on toast and several games of canasta. I moved along in it as though I was walking through fog. And in a way, I was. The mist all around us seemed to have totally clouded my thoughts. Or perhaps it was more to do with the fact that my world as I knew it was collapsing around me. The sadness Mr Beeston had left me with felt like a physical weight dragging me down.

The night wasn't much better. It was filled with dreams about my parents, and about the castle. In one, I was swimming towards it as hard as I could. Mum and Dad were waiting for me there, but it kept getting further and further away. With every stroke, it became more distant, but it was calling me, willing me to find a way to get there. All around me, voices were urging me on. Then the ring on my finger turned into a knife and cut through the sea so I could walk there – but I had no feet. My tail flapped lifelessly on the ground for a moment, till the ring shone a beam that lifted me and carried me towards the castle. I had almost reached it – it was centimetres away. And then I woke up.

Panting and sweating, I got up and looked out through my porthole. Directly ahead of me, the castle loomed just as it had done in my dream, the mist flowing around its middle like a skirt. Its windows were black and closed like sleeping eyes. But as I stared, they seemed to brighten, shining at me, just at me. Blinking and glinting, it was as though they were spelling something out in a code I had yet to crack. I knew one thing for certain, though. I had to get to the castle.

It was early; too early for anyone else to be up. Even the sun hadn't risen yet. The sky was a deep purple. I crept out on to the deck and looked around. In the distance, the castle was almost hidden by the mist. Just the turrets were visible, reaching upwards, tall and dark and forbidding.

As I looked across, my chest burned. I felt the ring tight on my finger, the diamond smooth and bright. 'What is it?' I asked silently. 'What do you want?'

The ring didn't reply. Well, no, it was a ring. But as I closed my fingers around it and breathed in the salty air, I knew I had to try again. My dream had been telling me there was something waiting for me at the castle. I just knew it. The thought was too strong for me to ignore. I had to get there, and I had to go now. If I waited any longer, Millie would be up and there was no way she was going to let me out of her sight again. And it wasn't fair to keep dragging Shona off on my crazy stunts. I'd already got her into enough trouble. No, let her sleep.

I slipped into the water as quietly as I could. The sea rippled around me as my legs jerked and twitched, stiffening, sticking together, and finally stretching out to form my tail. What there was of it. Again, patches were missing all over. Fleshy white bits of my legs poked through the scales. As I moved, my tail felt taut and tight. It didn't bend properly. It was getting worse.

Never mind. Just get there. Determination drove me on, and I ducked my head under the water and swam.

But it was just like last time, and just like my dream. The more I swam, the further away the castle seemed to be.

I ploughed through the water as hard as I could, thrashing my tail with every bit of energy I had, stretching my arms as wide as they would reach, pushing myself further and faster with every stroke. But it was useless. I was getting nowhere.

Below me, the sea looked dark and unwelcoming.

Jagged rocks were piled on top of each other as though they had been dumped there and forgotten long ago. Small pockets of sandy seabed were dotted about in between. Tiny black fish darted away as I swam across them. A round yellow fish slid slowly in and out of the crevices like a submarine.

I came to the surface to catch my breath. I didn't seem to be able to stay underwater as long as usual. That must be the curse too. Where would this end?

No, I couldn't think about that. I couldn't think about anything. I just had to get to the castle. But it was as far away as ever.

As I flicked my tail to tread water, I looked at the ring. 'What do I do?' I said out loud. And this time, it did reply. Not with words, but with a feeling, like it had before. A feeling that seeped through me like heat filling my bones. A feeling of trust. I had to trust the ring. Just as it had done in my dream, if I gave in and let it guide me, it would get me to the castle.

So I did. I stopped trying. I stopped swimming, stopped pushing myself to get there faster or sooner – and instead, I listened to the ring. It felt as though I was tuning a radio: finding the right station and getting it clear and sharp enough to hear it properly.

I held my hand out in front of me, letting the ring guide me. Immediately, the water became smoother; a gentle current started to glide me along. With the slightest, tiniest flicks of my tail, I zoomed forwards. Heading towards the castle.

At last, it was coming closer! Soon the current slowed. The water seemed to grow thicker, and colder, and much darker.

Below me, a shoal of silver fish swirled down like a light beam, flashing briefly through the black sea. In their wake, a group of manta rays slowly flapped their long capes as they slithered by. I kept well out of the way, watching from behind a rock till they'd passed.

Ahead of me, the sea looked even blacker. As I got closer, I could see a big dark hole, a tunnel. Sharp rocks formed a ring around its entrance.

The strangest fish seemed to pace across the tunnel's entrance, gliding heavily and slowly. Five or six of them. I knew what these were. I'd never seen one in real life, but we'd studied them in Aquatics & Animals. Humphead parrotfish. Almost twice as big as me, they looked like big burly bouncers wearing silly masks and gum shields. Their bodies were grey, with a purple splodge of paint in a line up their heads, like mohicans, or war paint. These fish had jaws you didn't want to get in the way of. Each time one of them passed the tunnel's entrance, it opened its enormous mouth and took a bite at the rock, dissolving it into soft sand. A tiny beach lay around the entrance.

My tail shook. The castle lay beyond this tunnel. I knew it.

I waited for ages, counting the seconds in between each sweep of the tunnel's entrance until I'd worked out the best time to go. One more parrotfish passed the entrance – and then it was bare. This was it. They were all facing away, swimming to opposite sides. Any second now, one of them would turn and swim back. It was now or never. And never wasn't an option.

So I darted into the tunnel.

It was so cold in there, and so dark. And I felt so alone. Every now and then, I passed something. Thin black fish swam in single file along the sides of the tunnel, coming from behind and overtaking me. Thick chunky silvery-blue fish flopped by in pairs, swimming towards me and sailing over my head. Trails of seaweed hung from the walls, waving with the current and making me jump when they brushed against me.

I swam on.

The tunnel twisted and writhed about like a giant snake. *Round the next corner, round the next corner*, I said to myself again and again. It had to end some time.

And then it did.

The tunnel led upwards, growing lighter and

warmer with every stroke until I emerged, panting and breathless, into a round pool. I took a few seconds to catch my breath as I glanced around. Where was I?

I swam all round the edges of the pool. The walls were grey rock and covered in green algae, chunks of bubbly seaweed hanging down into the water like bunches of grapes on a vine.

Above water, the pool was enclosed by walls. Grey, lumpy, dark and cold, dripping with damp, it was like a long-forgotten cellar, with a metal door in one corner.

I'd done it. I was in the castle. In a cellar. On my own.

What was I *doing*?

I shivered as I pulled myself out of the water and waited on the side, watching my tail flicker half-heartedly, flapping on the surface of the water as it faded away. My legs slowly emerged, numb and tingling. This time the numbness in my feet didn't go away. I looked down. Webbed. Even more so, like my hands.

I didn't have time to think about that, or about any of the fears I could so easily think about if I gave myself half a chance. Just one question remained: Why was I so sure the castle offered me something? I tried to bat that question away with the rest of my dark thoughts. Whatever the castle wanted with me, I had to find out and get back to the boat. The others would be up soon.

Edging round to the doorway, I felt for a handle. A brass knob turned slowly, creaking like an ancient floorboard as I twisted it both ways. Despite the creaking, it turned easily enough, and I opened the door.

I inched my way up a spiral staircase, gripping a rope handrail for support. Round and round, the stairs climbed steeply and tightly. I felt as though I was climbing into the clouds, floating upwards. By the time I reached the top, I was dizzy and disorientated. Another door. This time I held my breath and turned the knob as slowly and gently as I could.

I was in a corridor, wide and long, with pictures all the way along the walls. Battle scenes, shipwrecks, storms at sea; the kind of thing you always see in castles like this.

I almost laughed at myself. Castles like this? How could I even think for a moment that this was like anywhere I'd ever been?

I mean, yes, from the inside it looked a bit like the kind of place your grandparents might visit on a Sunday afternoon. But there was something different about it, too. Apart from the fact that it seemed to float on a mist in the middle of the ocean, something about it felt unreal – like a film set or a cartoon. I couldn't put my finger on it exactly, but it was just a tiny step removed from reality. As I stepped along the corridor, I felt a bit like an actor in a film where everything except them is computer-generated animation. Unreal.

I kept glancing at the pictures to see if anything had changed while I looked away – whether the boats had moved, or the storms had raged while I wasn't looking. They didn't. Of course they didn't. I was imagining it. I must be.

I crept on down the corridor. Ahead of me, another door lay open. I went in.

It was a smallish, box-shaped room, jam-packed from floor to ceiling with dusty books in fancy bindings, all bronze and gold. The titles were full of words I could hardly read. Most were foreign, a few were English. All looked hundreds of years old. Not exactly your light-hearted bedtime reading.

Then I noticed the window. A large rectangle that covered half of one side of the room, it was set into a recess with a small bench. I sat on the bench and looked out. The sea stretched out for miles and miles, all the way to the horizon, just like it did from *Fortuna*. But down below, waves lapped on rocks that were gradually surfacing like bared teeth as the tide edged out. It was as though the castle stood on a podium above the rest of the world; separate from the world, floating above it as though in a dream. *What was this place?*

Another door took me out of the library into a smaller room. One side of the room was filled with weapons. Opposite, the wall was covered in silk banners painted with flags from all over the world. I recognised some of the shapes and colours from geography lessons back in Brightport. Others were completely unfamiliar. There was even a skull and crossbones on one flag.

I moved on quickly. The room led out to another corridor. More paintings on the walls, this time portraits. Men in naval uniforms, beautiful women smiling up at them, young men standing proud on the decks of warships, girls perched on rocks. I moved closer to examine the pictures in more detail. Hold on. Were they girls, or were they –

What was that?

A bell clanged loudly, echoing down the corridor.

I glanced furtively around. Was it me? Had I tripped an alarm? Was someone going to come out and catch me? *No! Please don't let me be captured again!* Memories rushed through me with a horrible judder, of being caught and imprisoned in an underwater cell after I'd woken the kraken. I couldn't get caught here!

There was a recess behind me, a heavy wooden

door at the back of it. I jammed myself up into it, my heart almost bursting out of my mouth. Pinning my body to the door, I held my breath, shut my eyes tight and prayed for the alarm to stop.

And then it did. Stopped dead. Silence, all along the long corridor. Nothing moved.

My body sagged in relief as I leaned against the door, letting out a long breath and trying to decide what to do next.

The relief didn't last long. A moment later, I heard footsteps. They were coming from behind the door, getting closer! There was no time to hide. My body froze as I stood in the recess.

And then the door opened.

Chapter Nine

J was looking into a pair of very green and very surprised eyes.

'Who are you?' asked the boy, staring back at me. He was tall, taller than me anyway, and skinny like me, too. He was probably about the same age, maybe a little older, and dressed in black flared trousers and a black T-shirt. He had long jet-black hair, parted perfectly in the middle, and the most piercing green eyes I'd ever seen, which he continued to fix seriously on me.

For a brief second, I remembered Millie's prediction about tall dark strangers. Was this him? What had she said about him? I couldn't remember. I tended not to listen carefully to Millie's fortune-telling. For once, I wished I had done.

'I – I – ' was all I managed to say.

The boy glanced quickly down the corridor before beckoning me into the room. 'You'd better come in,' he said. His voice was silky and smooth, like his hair, and serious like his face.

As I followed him into the room, I forced myself to speak. 'I'm Emily,' I said. I couldn't think of anything else to say. I looked awkwardly around me. Three of the walls were covered with maps and scrolls. There wasn't a blank centimetre. Every country and every ocean in the world must have been on these walls. The fourth wall had a long rectangular window that looked out to sea. Beneath it, a thick wooden bookcase held rows and rows of books, brown and bound in gold like the ones in the library. The room felt almost unreal, as though the books and maps were part of a stage set, and underneath them lay a thousand years of history and mystery.

The boy noticed me looking. 'They're from my ancestors,' he explained.

'Your ancestors?'

'Pirates, captains, travellers of all sorts,' he said. 'Many ships have been wrecked on the rocks of Halflight Castle.'

I nodded, as though I understood.

'Look, sit down,' he said, gesturing to a huge armchair. With its thick dark wooden arms and green velvet seat, it reminded me of the furniture in the stately homes I used to visit with Mum sometimes. Mum. Just the thought of her made me ache. Where was she now? Was she trying to find me? Would I ever see her again? Each question was like a knife twisting round and round in my chest.

The boy carried on staring at me as I sat down. He pulled up an identical chair and sat opposite me. 'I'm Aaron,' he said. He held out a skinny arm to shake my hand, but almost instantly changed his mind and pulled it away.

We fell silent. I didn't have the first idea what to say. Well, come on. How many times do you think about what you'll do if you swim to a spooky castle floating on a mist in the middle of the ocean and accidentally land yourself in some strange boy's room?

Exactly.

He was the first to pull himself out of the shocked silence. 'How did you get here?' he asked.

'Um, I swam,' I said uncertainly.

His eyes opened even wider. 'You swam?'

I nodded. 'Through tunnels. But where am I? What kind of a place is this?'

'Halflight Castle. It's my home,' said Aaron. 'I

don't know any other.'

'You've lived here all your life?'

He nodded. 'All my life. Here and nowhere else, like every generation before me, all the way back to . . . ' He looked up at me through his thick black eyelashes. 'No, I can't tell you that.'

'Can't tell me what?'

'My family history,' he replied with a grimace. 'It's not exactly straightforward. You'll never believe me.'

I laughed. 'You think *your* family history is hard to believe. Wait till you hear mine!'

He didn't smile. 'Trust me. It's complicated. Or it was. Nothing too complicated now though, as it's just Mother and me.'

'Just the two of you in this whole place?'

'And a few si – ' He stopped himself, covering whatever he was about to say with a cough.

'A few what?' I asked.

'Servants,' he said quickly.

'You weren't going to say that. What were you going to say?' I insisted.

Aaron shook his head and stood up. 'I don't think I can tell you,' he said. 'I'm not sure. Look, why don't you tell me about you instead? How *did* you get here? It's meant to be impossible.'

'It nearly was,' I said. 'I tried again and again.' Could I tell him about the ring? It was tight on my finger, the diamond warm against my closed palm.

I could feel it almost scorching my hand, getting hotter. What was it saying? Tell him? Or keep it to myself?

Why should I keep it secret anyway? I had nothing to hide. 'Look, if I tell you, you promise you'll believe me?'

'Why would I do otherwise? Why would you lie?'

'OK,' I said. 'Well, it was this. It kind of led me here.' I held my hand out and opened my palm. 'Now, I know you'll think I'm making it up or you'll think I'm mad or something but I promise I'm telling you the – '

'Where did you get that?' Aaron reached out and grabbed my hand, pulling it towards him to look more closely. His voice shook so much I could barely understand what he'd said. He swallowed hard, catching his breath. His face had turned even paler. 'Where did you get it?' he repeated.

'I – I found it,' I said uncertainly.

'Do you know what it is?' he asked.

'Well, I, yes, I think I do.' Did *he* know what the ring was? Had he heard of Neptune, heard the story?

'I've never seen it,' he said in a whisper. 'Not the real one!'

He fell silent, squeezing his mouth into a tight line and his eyes tightly closed while he thought. 'Right,' he said, making up his mind about something.

'We've got time. Come with me.'

With that, he motioned to me to follow him to the door. Glancing down the corridor again, he nodded back to me. 'Come on,' he said. 'I want to show you something.'

Aaron led me down a maze of corridors, scurrying quickly along till we came to a thick wooden door with bars and bolts across it. I followed him outside. Below us, the sea washed against rocks in the semi-darkness. We ran round the front of the castle and back inside through a small arched door. Following Aaron inside, I felt as though I was stepping further and further into a dream. Was any of this real? I mean, it *felt* real. The bricks of the castle were thick and hard, the rocks below were jagged and cold. But still, something in the atmosphere made me feel as though I was floating, suspended just above reality, as if the castle were floating on the mist.

I closed the door behind me.

We were in what looked like a small church, a tiny chapel in a remote wing of the castle. A few rows of seats all faced a raised platform at the front. Stained glass windows were filled with pictures of Biblical scenes.

I followed Aaron to the raised platform. Right at the back of it, there was a chest. He opened it. 'Look,' he said, pointing inside.

I peered into it. It contained a glass cabinet and, inside that, two rings. I looked more closely at the one on the left, comparing it with the ring on my finger. It was identical!

'But that's – but they're – '

'Imitations,' he said. 'My great-grandfather made them. From the descriptions, from the stories passed down through generation after generation.'

'What stories? What descriptions?' I asked, my head spinning. 'Do you mean about Neptune and Aurora?'

'You know?' he gasped. 'You know the story?'

'That's all I know,' I said. 'Please, tell me.'

Aaron moved away from the cabinet. 'When Neptune and Aurora married, they cast a spell on their rings. While they were held by a human and merperson who were in love – '

He glanced at me to check I understood what he meant, to check we were talking about the same thing. Maybe to check I didn't think he was ridiculous for believing in mermaids. *I don't only believe in them*, I thought. *I am one!* But I wasn't going to say that. Not yet. Not if it was just a story. Surely boys like him didn't really believe in mermaids!

I nodded for him to continue.

123

'As long as the rings were worn by one from the land and one from the sea who loved each other, there would always be harmony between the two worlds,' he went on. 'And there was. For the brief time the marriage lasted, there really was peace between land and sea. No ships were wrecked on rocks, no cargo was stolen, no sirens lured fishermen to their watery graves. Just peace. The two worlds thrived together. It was a magical time.'

'And then she left him,' I said, remembering what Shona had said about her history lesson.

Aaron's green eyes bore down on me. 'She *what?*' he asked angrily.

'She – she left him?' I said more uncertainly. 'Didn't she?'

'You know nothing!' he snapped. 'Believing in such rubbish. How dare you?'

I pulled at my hair, twisting it round my fingers. 'I'm sorry,' I said. 'I thought she did. I thought she broke his heart. I'm sorry.'

'She did not leave him,' Aaron said firmly. 'She loved him more than anything in the world. I'll tell you what her love for him drove her to do.'

I clamped my mouth shut. No more interruptions.

'She loved him so much, and believed so strongly in the magic they had created, that she attempted the impossible. One night, she decided

124

to show him what she could do out of love for him. You know what she did?'

I shook my head.

'She thought she could swim underwater to his palace. She believed their love was so great it surpassed the normal laws of her human world. She believed she could become a mermaid. She drowned.'

Neither of us spoke for a long time. As we stood in the silence, it felt as though the chapel was the whole world. That the sea outside the window was only there for us. We were somehow at the centre of everything, the centre of something so important that – that what? I couldn't tell.

'It was her birthday. She'd wanted to surprise him as her present to him,' Aaron went on. 'Her own birthday, and she wanted to surprise *him*. They'd only been married a year and a week.'

'Go on,' I said softly.

'When Neptune found her body, he took the ring from her and – '

'I know this bit,' I said quickly – even if it wasn't exactly how Mr Beeston had told it! I had to get it right this time; show him he could trust me. 'He tore the pearl ring from her finger and threw away his own ring, the diamond one.'

'That's right,' Aaron said. 'And no one has ever seen the rings – till now.' He fell silent.

'The kraken had Neptune's ring,' I said. 'I found it.'

Aaron stepped towards me. 'Emily, these rings can only be worn by certain folk.'

'I know,' I said, swallowing.

'A human and merperson in love, or a child of theirs . . . ' His voice trailed off into a question mark.

I didn't reply. Finally, I nodded.

'I thought as much,' Aaron said, suddenly smiling. 'You're a semi-mer! You are, aren't you?'

'How did you know?'

'You said you swam here through the tunnels. No human can swim underwater that far. It's impossible.' He grinned wider. His whole face changed with his smile; it was like watching a two-dimensional picture come to life. 'You found the diamond ring!' he said. 'You really found it!'

'Why is that so great?' I asked.

Aaron led me back to the glass cabinet. 'Look,' he said, pointing to an inscription written in black swirly writing beneath the rings. I read aloud. 'When the rings touch, they will overrule any act born of hatred or anger. Only love shall reign.'

I looked up at Aaron. 'I don't understand,' I said.

'There's a curse,' he answered me, his face darkening. 'It must be undone. And soon.'

'What curse?'

Aaron brushed my question away with a flick of his hand. 'We still need to find the pearl ring, though,' he said. 'And that's impossible.'

'Who says it's impossible? I found this one!' I said, my breath tripping over my words as it raced into my throat.

'The second ring will be much harder to find. The one Neptune ripped from Aurora's finger. He swore it could only be found when it was seen under the light of a full moon. But there was a catch.'

'A catch?'

'The ring was buried so deep it has never seen the moon's light. And so it has never been found. Neptune and Aurora married under a full moon on the spring equinox, at midnight. At that moment, the sea's tide is the lowest it will ever be – and only then is it low enough for the ring to be visible. But those conditions only occur every five hundred years. It's virtually impossible to find it. We'll never stop the curse.'

'What curse?' I asked again.

Aaron walked to a small recess. His breath misted the window pane as he looked out. 'After Aurora died, Neptune turned to hatred and anger. There were storms for years. Ships were wrecked at sea. Many fishermen died, many humans perished in the seas over the years that followed. But even that wasn't enough for Neptune. Even that couldn't take away his rage.'

'So what did he do?'

'First, he banned any more marriages between humans and merfolk. He swore the two worlds would never again live in harmony.'

Well, yes, I knew all about *that*. 'And second?' I asked.

'Neptune and Aurora had three children,' said Aaron. 'Two sons and a daughter.'

'What happened to them?'

'In his grief and sorrow, Neptune cursed them,' he went on. 'His own children. Each of his own children, and their children and every generation that followed, every single one of them would die young, and always on Aurora's birthday, as she did. He couldn't forgive her – and because of this, her family would forever be punished.'

'His family too,' I said.

Aaron nodded. 'Their family. And there was another curse placed on them. They would never fit in, never be of one world or the other. They would be not quite human, not quite merperson. Whichever form they took, it would always be held back by remnants of their other form. Every single generation forever would be the same. Do you understand?'

Did I understand? If only he knew how well I understood! 'Aaron. Look!' I thrust my hands in front of his face, opening my fingers so he could see how they were webbed.

'You too?' he said simply. 'You're the same.'

I nodded.

'The only way to undo these curses would be to bring the rings together again,' said Aaron.

'Because the curse came from hatred and anger,' I said, finally understanding the significance of what I had found. We just had to find the other ring and we could end the curse on his family! And end the curse on me, too! I could carry on being a semi-mer! I'd never have to lose my parents! The thought sent my hopes soaring. Till Aaron spoke again.

'But that will almost certainly never happen,' he said. 'The chance will only come once every five hundred years.'

'When was the marriage?'

'No one knows for sure. It must be about five hundred years ago, though. It could be more. The moment has probably already passed. So the curses will remain forever, and nothing will ever bring back harmony between land and sea.'

Aaron fell silent. His words spun round and round in my head. I'd found one ring. Why couldn't we find the other?

'Where was it buried?' I asked suddenly. 'The second ring. Where was it buried?'

'Right where she died. Just beyond her home.'

Aaron ran a hand through his sleek hair.

'Her home?' I asked. I was pretty sure what he was going to say. Pretty sure he wasn't just telling me any old story. Someone else's story. I was pretty sure it was his story. That her home was his home, her family was his.

'Yes,' he said. 'She lived here at Halflight Castle. In fact, Neptune had the castle built especially for her, for them. A place of magic and beauty and love where their two worlds came together. And ever since, it's been a symbol of the exact opposite, keeping every generation separate from the rest of the world.'

'Completely separate? Don't you ever see anyone else?'

'There has been more life here, at different points in the castle's history. But it's never been a happy place since that time. And with the curses, the family's dwindled more and more over the years. It's just me and Mother now. We have a few visitors who bring us our supplies but they hardly talk to us.'

'Why not?'

'Mostly they're sirens, employed by Neptune. They daren't go against Neptune's rule. They're all instructed not to talk to us, although there are a few who I'm secretly friends with,' Aaron said. 'It's a pretty lonely life,' he added.

Sirens! That's what he was going to say earlier,

when he changed it to servants. I knew it! And I was right about Aaron being descended from Neptune and Aurora too! Before I had a chance to say anything, the alarm sounded again, crashing into every bit of space around us, filling my head with noise.

Aaron jumped as though he'd been stung. 'Mother,' he said. 'I forgot!'

'What is it?' I called over the din.

'It's my mother. She's confined to bed. She rings it when she needs me. I didn't go to her earlier. Emily, I have to leave.' Aaron hurried to the door. Outside the chapel, waves crashed against the rocks. The sky was starting to grow light; above the mist, clouds were turning pink, anticipating the day ahead. Cobwebs shone brightly in the doorframe. Elaborate spiralling mazes in one corner, half-finished scraps and threads dangling loosely in another, gaping and half-empty like derelict houses.

'Quick. Go back to the tunnels. It's the only way. It's too dangerous on the rocks.' Aaron led me back to the door that would take me back down to the cellar. 'Down there,' he said, opening it and virtually shoving me inside. 'You'll find your way back?'

'Yes, of course.'

'Come back soon!' he said urgently. '*Promise* me!'

'I promise,' I said.

'Good.' He allowed himself a brief smile. 'I have to go now.' And with that, he closed the door and left me in the darkness.

Chapter Ten

*L*owering myself down, I made my way smoothly back to the cellar and set off towards *Fortuna*. Heading back didn't feel half so difficult. The current drew me along. The ring vibrated in my hand, buzzing warmly. It seemed as excited as I was! It was willing me to get back to Shona and tell her everything.

As I swam, I watched the sky changing, moment by moment, the clouds growing orange and bright. The sun rose in front of me, shining hard into my eyes as though it was a weapon sent to blind me.

Beneath it, the mist rolled along the top of the sea like a thin layer of snow. *Don't let Millie be up yet*, I said to myself, swimming as hard as I could to get back, despite my tail feeling as though it was made from iron, and despite my breath coming out in rasps, shorter and shorter with every stroke.

The second I swam through the porthole, Shona was there.

'Where have you *been*?' she whispered fiercely.

'Is Millie up?'

'No.' She shook her head. 'I couldn't sleep and I was calling you. I figured you must have still been asleep.'

'Shona. I got there,' I said. 'I got to the castle!'

Shona whistled. 'Flipping fins! How? What's it like? Did you go inside? Does anyone live there?'

I laughed, holding up my hands to ward off any more questions. 'I'll tell you everything,' I said. 'Just let me get my breath back.'

Shona listened in silence to the whole story. When I'd finished, she simply stared at me.

'What?' I asked.

'Emily, you have to find the other ring. It's your only hope!'

'I know – but I can't. It's impossible. No one's seen it for hundreds of years. It's buried too deep. It's not suddenly going to turn up now!'

Shona bowed her head. 'We have to find it, Emily. We have to find a way. We can't give up.

There's too much to lose.'

'You're telling me!' Shona wasn't even the one with something to lose. I was going to lose the whole of the mermaid world, or the whole of my life as I'd known it up until now. Mr Beeston's words hadn't left my mind for a second. Neptune's law. I would see my parents on the night of the full moon, one of them for the last time ever. And I didn't even know which one.

'And before you say I've got nothing to lose,' Shona said, reading my mind as usual, 'I have. I've got *you* to lose. And I'm not prepared to let that happen. Right?'

I let myself smile at my best friend. 'Right,' I said.

We stared out at the castle. It seemed to be staring back at us, the mist curling around its base like a dark blanket, the turrets bright and harsh in the sun, the windows shining like lights.

'We can find it,' Shona insisted quietly as she swam towards me and grabbed my hand. 'Emily, you can end the curse! You just need to bring the rings back together. You'll change Aaron's life as well!'

'Maybe it'll bring harmony back to sea and land too,' I said excitedly. Before I could stop myself, I added, 'And then Neptune would change his mind and Mum and Dad could carry on being together!'

Then I stopped. My shoulders slumped and I sank lower in the water as I thought about what I was saying. What if Mum and Dad didn't even *want* to be together? The way things had been lately, they would probably be happy with Neptune's new law! And then there was of course the fact that the ring was buried so deep it would never be seen.

I was going to lose a parent. It would happen just as Mr Beeston had told us. When the full moon came, Neptune would bring my parents to me and I would say goodbye to one of them – forever. The thought was so dark and so huge, it felt as if I was falling into it, into the deep chasm that was my future. I stroked the gold band on my finger, pressed the diamond against my palm, looking for comfort, but it felt cold. It had no comfort to offer me.

'Who am I kidding?' I said, my words as heavy as my heart. 'We're not going to find the ring. We'll never stop all these terrible things happening.'

'We will NOT give up!' Shona said, swimming round in front of my face and lifting my chin just like Mum does when she forces me to listen. 'Do you hear me?' she said sternly. 'That is not my best friend talking. The one who explores shipwrecks and caves and breaks into prisons to rescue her dad! We'll find a way. Right?'

I nodded gratefully. 'OK,' I said. She was right. I couldn't give up. I couldn't just let my life slip away, lose a parent, lose half of what I was. Being a mermaid wasn't just something I did for fun. It was part of who I *was*. I couldn't lose that. We *had* to find the other ring and bring the two together. Then anything born of anger and hatred would end. The curse on me would have to be lifted, and the curse on Aaron, too. He could have a completely new life. Perhaps he and his mum could even come to Allpoints Island with us! We *had* to find the ring. It was as simple as that.

'OK,' I said again. 'We need to find out when the full moon is. That's how long we've got till the curse on me is complete. As soon as the full moon has passed, that's it. I won't be a semi-mer any more and Neptune will take back his ring.'

'And I may never see you again,' Shona said quietly.

We both looked down in silence. Below me, a couple of black and yellow striped fish darted into the boat like lovers running away together. They swam off to the other end of the boat, leaving the sea fans waving gently behind them.

Just then, a shuffling noise above us made us both glance up. Millie's face appeared at the trapdoor. 'Ah, you're awake,' she said. 'I was just going to make some breakfast. You coming?'

'We'll be right up,' I said. Conversation closed, for now.

I munched slowly on my one piece of toast. I had to make the most of it; I wouldn't get anything else till lunchtime, and even then it wouldn't be enough to satisfy the gnawing in my stomach. I didn't know if it was just hunger or the pain of missing my parents so much. Either way, it hurt.

Millie sipped her tea. 'Not the same without milk,' she murmured. 'I can't be doing with too much bergamot.' She winced as she put her cup down. 'So, what shall we do today?' she asked, almost brightly. She sounded as though we were on a package holiday and just had to decide between the pool, the beach or the trip to see the dolphins. 'I thought we might try a bit of dowsing,' she added before we had a chance to reply. 'It could help us to work out where we are.'

'What's dowsing?' I asked.

Millie closed her eyes and drew a heavy breath. Gathering her cloak around her, she held her hands up to her chest. 'Dowsing,' she said breathily, her voice husky and deep, 'is the harnessing of the senses – or, more precisely, of the sixth sense.'

'The sixth sense?' Shona said. 'I thought we only had five senses.'

'Intuition, my dear,' Millie replied, briefly opening an eye to glance at Shona. 'The ability to dowse is something I firmly believe to be within us all,' she went on. 'Most of us do not know a fraction of what we can do. For too many of us, our intuition is ignored or relegated to some backwater of the mind. But it's there. It's all there.' She fell silent, nodding gently as she breathed heavily and slowly.

Her eyes closed, she held her hands out in front of her, palms facing up. 'Dowsing is often used to find water, but it can do so much more.' She glanced at our blank faces before continuing. 'In layman's terms, it is a way of tuning into sources of spiritual power, harnessing nature's own resources just as the chakras harness the powers within our bodies.'

'Mm,' I said, not following a word.

After a few more deep breaths, her eyes snapped open and she sat up straight. 'Right then,' she said, smiling at us both. 'We just need a Scrabble set and a couple of coat-hangers and we're sorted.' And with that, she got up and went inside.

Shona and I took one look at each other and burst out laughing. 'You'll get used to her,' I said. 'Just look as though you know what she's going on about and you'll be fine.'

'But she's got a point,' Shona said.

'What? About the dowsing?'

She shook her head. 'The stuff she said about harnessing nature's energy. That's what we need to do.'

'Harnessing nature's energy?' I said. 'You're getting as bad as Millie!'

'Emily, we need to use anything we can think of if we're to find this ring,' Shona said crossly.

Millie had joined us back out on the deck before I had a chance to reply.

'It's the perfect time to do this,' Millie said, scattering the Scrabble letters on the deck and bending the wire into a new shape. 'I don't know why I didn't think of it earlier.'

'Perfect time?' I said. 'What's perfect about it?' What could she possibly see as being perfect about *anything* right now?

'Magical time,' she said with a wink. 'Spring equinox some time around now.'

'The spring equinox?' I asked, remembering what Aaron had said. The tide was at its lowest point of the year. A brief spark of hope flickered – but went out almost as fast as it had come when I remembered what he'd said next. That there would only be one year when the tide was low enough – and that time had probably already passed.

'In fact . . . ' Millie was saying as she reached into the little bag she always carried on her shoulder. She pulled out a small book. It was bound in black felt with pink and blue feathers around the edges and 'Orphalese Oracle' spelt out in fancy letters along the spine. 'If I remember rightly, this year is even *more* special.'

'Even more special?' Shona asked, her voice tight and high. 'Why is it even more special?'

'Let me check.' Millie looked through her book, licking her thumb and flicking through the pages. 'Aha! Yes, that's it,' she smiled. 'It *is* extra special! This year the full moon and spring equinox are at exactly the same time. The same day. And my word! Fancy that!'

'What?' I asked, my nerves about to crash and splinter.

'The full moon falls at midnight!'

I swallowed hard. 'At *midnight*?' I asked, my voice quivering like a freshly caught fish. 'Are you sure?'

'Absolutely!' Millie snapped. She tapped the cover of her book. 'Emily, you'd be sensible not to doubt the word of the Orphalese Oracle. Never been wrong yet, in my experience.' She tutted loudly and went back to flicking through the book, squinting and mumbling under her breath. 'Full moon at midnight,' she muttered. 'I bet that doesn't happen often.'

Happen *often*? How about once every five hundred years! This was *it*! This year – the one chance to find the ring!

'Millie, can I see?'

She passed me the book. My hands shook so much the words started to blur. But I saw all I needed to see. She was right! The full moon was at midnight on the spring equinox! My hands shook so much when I read the next bit that I nearly dropped the book. The date! It was tonight.

I handed the Orphalese Oracle back to Millie in silence. I couldn't make any words come out of my throat.

'*Very* interesting,' Millie said, oblivious to the change in mood as she smiled at us both. Then she put the book back in her bag and picked up the coat-hanger. 'Now, let's see about this dowsing.'

'That's odd,' Millie said, frowning in concentration as she waved her coat-hanger over the Scrabble letters.

'What? Has it told you where we are?' I asked, edging closer to watch over her shoulder.

Millie shook her head. 'It keeps moving over to you.' She glanced at me. 'To your hands. As though it wants to tell us something about the ring. Watch. It's telling me there's a strong connection between the ring and ... hold on. It's spelling something out.'

I watched her waggle the coat-hanger over the letters. It didn't look as if it was doing anything except twitching and wiggling in her hands.

'Something about a star,' Millie mumbled as the coat-hanger moved across the letters.

Shona hitched herself higher on the side of the deck. 'Stars? Maybe it's telling us to use the stars to find our way back.'

'No, it's definitely to do with the ring. A strong link with the ring and – hold on. It's not finished,' Millie said, following the coat-hanger's progress and reading aloud. 'Star – l – i – '

'Starlight?' I suggested.

'Could be. Wait.' We all watched the coat-hanger intensely as it moved to the letter 'n', then 'g', then 's'. After that, it stopped twitching and lay still in Millie's hands.

'Starlings!' Millie said eventually, pulling a hanky out from her bag and wiping her forehead as she put the coat-hanger down.

'Starlings?' I repeated blankly. 'What have starlings got to do with anything?'

Why? Why had I gone and done it again? Believing that Millie's so-called psychic intuition might bear any resemblance to anything that made any sense. Why?

'I don't know, love.' Millie sounded as flat as me. 'It sometimes takes a few attempts to work properly. Needs warming up, you know. Why don't you run along for now and we'll give it another go later?'

Shona and I slunk away and left her to it.

'So much for dowsing!' I said, dropping into the water beside her. My tail flickered half-heartedly to life, as weak and limp as the few shreds of hope I still had. The full moon was tonight. If we didn't find the ring, the curse would be full. By tomorrow I would have lost a parent.

'Come on, Em. Aaron said the tide would be at its lowest point for five hundred years tonight!'

'But what if he's wrong?' I said. 'The curse ends tonight. Neptune will take the ring. It's all over.' I couldn't bear it — couldn't even think through to the end of the thought. My future was a black hole, and at midnight I would slip into it.

'You have to believe him,' Shona said. Her voice was so full of hope, I couldn't help letting her enthusiasm filter across to me. My heart filled like a tight balloon.

'You're right,' I said with new determination. 'It's the only chance we're going to get and we can't afford to miss it. We've got to find that ring — tonight!'

Chapter Eleven

'**B**e careful,' Shona whispered as she waved me off from the porthole. 'And good luck.'

'You too,' I said with a hopeful smile. 'See you soon.'

'You're sure you don't want me to come with you?'

'I'm sure,' I said. We'd agreed I had to go straight back to the castle and tell Aaron the news. There was no time to lose. Shona was going to stay behind and fend Millie off if she came looking for us. Thankfully, she'd become so absorbed in her dowsing that she wouldn't notice any-thing for a while. I wouldn't have long, though. The last thing I wanted was for her to worry about me, on top of everything else. Or to keep a closer eye on me and stop me going out tonight. That was unthinkable! I'd just have to be careful – and quick.

I swam off in the same direction, listened to the ring in the same way, sneaked into the tunnel, and finally came up in the pool in the castle's cellar. I pulled myself out of the water and sat on the side to get my breath back. Panting and exhausted, I wondered how many more times I'd be able to get across here. My body was getting weaker by the hour. My tail was get-ting more patchy, my breathing more scratchy. *Just one more day. Please let me hold out for one more day.*

I heard a noise creak behind me, and leapt to my feet.

'Emily!' It was Aaron! Still dressed all in black, his hair was tied back in a sleek ponytail; his face shone pale and clear in the semi-darkness of the cellar.

'I've been hanging around here since you left,' he said, softly closing the door behind him. 'I was hoping you'd come back.'

'I said I would.'

Aaron took a step nearer the pool, and that's

when I noticed something. His feet – they were webbed. Of course they were. He was descended from Aurora, which meant the curse affected him too. Like me, he was stuck between the two worlds, neither fully one thing nor another.

He noticed me looking and shyly held out a hand. 'Come on, let me help you out of the pool,' he said. This time he didn't snatch his hand away. He held it out, palm upwards, fingers outstretched. Showing me. His fingers were joined at the knuckle by the thinnest wafer-like stretches of skin. His hands were webbed too. As I reached up to grab his hand, it was as though we were shaking on a deal. We were the same. We were in this together.

We sat on the side of the pool. Aaron stared as my tail melted away and my legs reformed.

'I can't even do that properly,' he said. 'My legs stick together and my toes flap about a bit, but that's all.' He looked at me wistfully. 'Just as it's been for the rest of my family, every generation.'

'Aaron, we can change it,' I said. 'That's what I've come to tell you. It's tonight. The full moon – it's at midnight!'

Aaron's eyes widened. 'Tonight? This is the year? How do you know?'

I told him about Millie and the Orphalese Oracle. I didn't mention the fact that Millie didn't always get it exactly right. She had to be right this time. She *had* to be.

'I don't believe it,' Aaron said, again and again. 'I don't believe it. Every spring equinox since I knew about it, I've hoped and wished. I've even searched for the ring, myself, and prayed the other one would somehow turn up.'

'I can't believe I ended up here,' I said, looking at the ring on my finger and smiling. I could feel its warmth smile back at me. 'I know I've had some lucky breaks in my life, but surely that's about as much of a coincidence as you can get.'

Aaron shook his head. 'It's not a coincidence at all,' he said. 'The ring brought you here.'

'Brought me to the castle?'

'The rings were meant to be together. When one is worn by a semi-mer, it wants to find the other one. While buried, the rings have no power. But when they are free, they want to be together. They're meant to be together. Its own heart brought you here.'

We fell silent, lost in our own thoughts, and maybe in our own hopes. 'Now we just have to find the pearl ring,' he said after a while.

'Not just find it. We have to find it and bring the two rings together under the full moon. It'll be too late after that. As soon as the full moon's passed, I won't be a semi-mer. I'll lose the ring again.'

'And if we fail . . . ' Aaron looked away as his voice failed.

'I lose a parent,' I said.

'So do I, Emily,' he said, his voice hardening.

'Huh?'

Aaron took a breath. 'Some years ago, life wasn't too bad here at the castle. Generations before me, it was a busy place. Years of ships wrecked on the rocks meant that occasionally the survivors found their way here. As I told you, Neptune has always installed sirens and some mermen to keep the castle isolated. So I've always at least had *some* company. Much to Neptune's disgust, there has always been love here, too. There has always been marriage, always been a determination to cross the forbidden boundaries.'

'Between land and sea?'

Aaron nodded and went on. 'But with every generation, it was the same. Just as I told you this morning, each one held the same fate. Each died young. The curse lived on from generation to generation. And still does, all these generations on.'

I didn't know what to say. I reached out to touch Aaron's arm.

He looked at my hand on his arm, then looked up at me. 'Father was the son of a ship's captain. He swore he would stop the curse before it affected my mother. No one ever knows exactly which year it will happen – only that it's always on the day of Aurora's birthday.' He glanced up at me. 'It's her side of the family that's descended from Neptune and Aurora.'

'Go on,' I prompted.

'There's not much to say. He tried to find the ring, and he failed. He searched and searched out there, but those rocks aren't kind, Emily.'

'What happened?'

'He drowned.'

'I'm so sorry,' I said quietly.

'It was three months ago,' he added, and I suddenly wondered if that was why he dressed so strangely, all in black. He was in mourning.

He turned back to face me, his eyes shining. 'That's why we've got to stop this, Emily. Even if the chances of succeeding are tiny, we have to try. We *have* to. This will be the only chance of our lives, and the only way to stop us both losing another parent.'

'Another parent? But – '

'My mother, Emily,' he interrupted. 'She's dying. It's Aurora's birthday next week. This is it.'

That was when I really understood that this wasn't just about me. It was about life and death. Literally. If we didn't find the ring, Aaron's mum was going to *die* next week, on Aurora's birthday, exactly as her ancestors had done.

'That's why she's confined to bed now. She's already ill. She only has a few days.' Aaron's voice juddered to a halt.

'We'll find the ring,' I said firmly. 'I promise.'

Aaron tried to smile, but even though he twitched his mouth up at the corners, his eyes were still the saddest I'd ever seen in my life. 'Come on,' he said, lowering himself into the water. 'I need to show you something I've just discovered. After you left, I went to see Mother, but meeting you had got me thinking. I went back to the chapel and dug around a bit more. Emily, I found something I'd never noticed before. Come and see it.'

I followed him back to the chapel.

'Through here.' Aaron guided me to the back of the chapel. At the end of the last row of seats, a few steps led down to a tiny gap, just big enough for us both to stand in.

Aaron felt around along the wall. He pushed it firmly and the wall creaked – and moved! A hidden door!

I followed him into a dark box of a room.

I looked round, blinking as my eyes grew accustomed to the darkness. Sunlight seeped in from the smallest gaps in the walls, just enough to see round the room: a small rectangle, with a long wooden bench all the way up one side, and an arched door opposite.

'I never knew it was here,' Aaron said, motioning for me to follow him. 'Look, I'll show you something strange.'

I stumbled across the dark room, my legs trembling with fatigue. Cobwebs filled every corner. I shivered as I followed Aaron to the far end of the room.

A row of paintings lined the wall, just as they lined the corridors all round the castle. 'More pictures,' I said.

Except that these were different. These weren't portraits, or pictures of battle scenes, and they weren't in frames either. They were murals, painted on the walls.

'It's all I've got. Pictures, books and maps from all round the world. That's my life. That's my school, my history, everything. But none like these.' He pointed to the first picture.

Now my eyes had grown accustomed to the darkness, I studied the painting. A deep blue sky, churning sea, and a bright white moon shining down on the castle.

'Who painted them?' I asked.

'I don't know. I bet it was my great-grandfather though,' said Aaron.

'The one who made the rings in the cabinet?'

He nodded. 'He was obsessed with the curse,

with trying to end it. The men in my family always are. These pictures seem like a clue.'

'They are,' I said, not even knowing why. The ring burned on my finger. It was the ring that knew the truth. 'They are a clue,' I repeated. 'I'm sure of it.'

'A secret clue, hidden from sight.'

'But why would someone want to pass on a message in secret?' I asked. 'If he was obsessed, why not tell everyone?'

'The only reason I can think of is so Neptune would never know.'

'But why not act on it, do something about it?'

'He probably didn't know what it meant any more than we do. But he knew it meant *something*. Look.' Aaron pointed at words scrawled all over the walls, painted around the pictures as though revealing the inner workings of the artist's mind. *'Why?' 'What is the significance?' 'How many years?'* the words said.

'Someone's been asking all the same questions as we have,' I said.

'And clearly had about as many answers as us,' Aaron replied flatly. 'Or else we wouldn't be in this position now.'

I stepped forward to study the first painting more closely. It was only then that I noticed the shadows in the sky. The swirling patterns looked familiar. A dark spinning cone in the sky.

Aaron moved to the next picture and motioned for me to follow. It was similar to the first. The same boiling sea, the sky even darker this time, the moon reflecting on to the rocks like a beam from a torch. The swirling shapes were there in the sky again. One looked like a spinning beehive, another like a dark trail from a plane that had been looping the loop.

'There's one more,' Aaron said, pointing to the third picture. It showed grey shining rocks, and the base of the castle. The swirling patterns were now just one thick black swarm: a whirlwind, its base at the tips of the rocks, in the centre of a shining white circle of light.

'I've seen these shapes!' I blurted out. 'The first night we were here! What are they?'

'I've seen them too. Usually at this time of year. It's birds. They come in their millions.'

'At this time of year? The spring equinox. But Aaron, that's proof! They *must* have something to do with the rings! And your great-grandfather knew it too.'

'I think you're right,' Aaron said. 'But the thing none of us knows is − what are they telling us?'

I wasn't aware of whether he said anything else. I was too busy staring at the words I'd just noticed among the rest, in capitals and underlined, like a title for the paintings.

My eyes glazed over, cold shivers running like electricity up and down the length of my body as I read the words: *THE STARLINGS*.

Chapter Twelve

I don't know how I got through the rest of the day. Shona and I scurried away every chance we got, to talk about what I had to do and how it was going to work out.

We swam round the lower half of the boat.

'Right, so you have to get to the castle, find the other ring and bring the two of them together,' Shona said, going over the plans for what felt like the twentieth time.

No matter how many times we repeated what I had to do, it wasn't sounding any easier.

'All in the few moments that the moon is full,' I said. 'Or it'll be too late. Neptune made his message clear enough. When the moon is full, the curse on me will be complete. I won't be a semi-mer any longer. And that means I won't even be able to touch the ring. I'll lose it forever.' *Along with everything else I care about,* I added silently.

Shona looked at me, holding my eyes with hers. 'Let's not think like that,' she said.

'I'll lose a parent,' I went on, ignoring her.

'Emily, please don't.'

'And Aaron will be an orphan.'

'Emily!' Shona took me by the shoulders. 'Concentrate. We can do this, OK?'

'OK,' I said lamely. I didn't believe for a minute that we could. The odds were just so highly stacked against us.

The sun had disappeared. This was it. A few more hours and the moon would rise into the sky. The full moon.

Millie wouldn't leave us alone. She stood on the front deck, pointing out the constellations as the stars appeared, one by one, across the vast sky.

'There's Canis Minor,' Millie said, pointing at a clutch of stars that looked pretty much exactly the same as all the others. 'And, oh, I think that might be the Corona Borealis.' She consulted her book, then looked back up at the sky. 'Yes, I think it is,' she went on, oblivious to whether anyone was actually listening. 'Well, you don't often get the chance to see that,' she said.

I smiled politely at her when she called me over, making all the right noises so she'd think I had some idea of what she was wittering on about. All I actually cared about was how I was going to get away from the boat before the moon came up. I glanced at my watch. Nearly ten o'clock. Two hours.

I tried feigning huge yawns, in the hope it would catch on and make her sleepy.

'Why don't you go to bed if you're tired?' was all she said.

Shaking my head in despair, I went to find Shona.

'What are we going to do?' I asked. 'I can't get away while she's out on the deck. We're going to run out of time.'

'Why don't you just tell her what you want to do?' Shona asked.

'I can't. She's already said again this evening she's not going to let me out of her sight. I'm not going to chance it. If only I could hypnotise her or something, like she does to other people.'

'Hey,' Shona said, a slow smile creeping across

her face. 'I might just have an idea.'

She rummaged around in her school bag. 'Ta da!' she said, producing her best B & D hairbrush. The handle was made from brass, and cast in the shape of a seahorse, the bristles soft and feathery like the prettiest horse's tail. On the back, there was a mirror, surrounded by pink shells.

'A hairbrush?' I said. 'Shona, this is no time to worry about what we look like! We've got a matter of hours!'

'I'm not worrying about what I look like!' Shona said crossly. 'Listen. I've got a plan.'

As she explained her idea, I couldn't help smiling, too. 'Shona, you're a marvel,' I said. 'It might just work.'

Millie was only too happy to oblige when I asked if she'd hypnotise me. 'It's just that I'm so tired, but I can't get to sleep,' I said. 'I need something to help me. I think your hypnotism is the only thing powerful enough to do the trick.'

She giggled and blushed. 'Oh, get away with you, pet,' she said. But she flicked her shawl importantly over her shoulder as I followed her into my bedroom.

I glanced at the chair I'd set up for Millie by my bed, hoping she wouldn't move it. It was perfectly positioned, as was the hairbrush on the dressing table. As long as she sat down without moving anything, the mirror should be in exactly the right spot to reflect her hypnotism right back on to her.

'Right then,' she began, settling herself down in the chair. Perfect! I lay on my bed and half closed my eyes. 'As you know, this is a powerful tool, so you may find you sleep even more deeply and soundly than usual,' she said. 'And you may find your dreams are more intense or elaborate. Don't worry about any of this. All that matters is you have a good long rest. Now, make yourself nice and comfy and we'll get started.'

I fidgeted around for a moment, trying to act as if I was getting myself comfortable. All I hoped was that I wouldn't get too comfortable and fall asleep.

What if it doesn't work? a voice in my head wouldn't stop asking. I did everything I could to ignore it. It simply *had* to work. There was no alternative.

Moments later, Millie was drawling in a deep, low voice about how tired I was getting. 'Imagine you are a feather,' she intoned, 'falling gradually down to the ground. With each breath, you sway a little bit lower, getting closer and closer to sleep.'

I couldn't help yawning. *Don't think about the feather, don't think about sleep,* I urged myself. *Think about what you have to do. Think about your mum, about your dad, about your one chance of getting them back together.*

That was all I needed. I was wide awake. And panicking so much it felt as if a high-speed train was racing through my chest.

'You're sleepy,' Millie drawled, even more slowly. 'Very . . . sleepy . . . ' Her voice was starting to sound as if she was drunk. 'In fact, you are so . . . very . . . sleepy . . . that you can't even . . . think . . . any more.' She took a deep breath and yawned a very loud yawn before continuing. 'All you want is to go to sleep.' A long pause. 'Beautiful sleep . . . ' An even longer pause. She yawned again. 'Peaceful . . . deep . . . '

This time the pause stretched on and on until a brief snort erupted through her nose. I waited a few more moments before daring to open an eye.

I had to clap a hand over my mouth to stop myself bursting out laughing. Millie lay sprawled across the chair, her legs spread out in front of her, her head thrown back, mouth wide open, eyes closed.

I quickly sat up on my bed. Carefully edging past Millie, I crept to the trapdoor in the middle of my floor, and lowered myself down.

'We did it!' I whispered excitedly to Shona. 'She's completely out.'

'Swishy!' Shona grinned. 'Come on. Let's go.'

We swam to the porthole and listened one more time. Nothing. This was it then.

'Wait,' I said. My tail hadn't finished forming. It was taking longer and longer. My legs had stuck together, but there were hardly any scales. I couldn't feel my legs – but I couldn't feel my tail either. It was as though there was nothing there at all. The whole bottom half of my body felt completely numb.

For a second, I panicked. What was going on? Had I become paralysed? Maybe I'd never walk *or* swim again!

Eventually, my tail formed, what there was of it. Bluey-green shiny scales at the ends, fleshy white skin almost all the way down to my knees. It felt wooden and inflexible, flicking half-heartedly in the water. My breathing was raspy. I don't know if Millie's hypnotism had anything to do with it or if it was just the curse, but by the time we swam out through the porthole, I was so exhausted I could almost have fallen asleep in the water.

Shona swam ahead, her tail splashing shiny droplets that sparkled in the moonlight. Would I ever do that again? Not that I ever swam as gracefully as Shona anyway. My heart felt as heavy as the rest of me.

'Wait,' I called, struggling to catch my breath.

Shona slowed. 'We've got to hurry,' she said. 'We haven't got long. The moon'll be up within the hour.'

'I know. I'm doing my best. I just – can't – keep up,' I gasped.

Shona swam beside me and took hold of my hand. 'Come on, Emily,' she said softly. 'You can do it. You've got me. We'll do it.'

I didn't reply. No point wasting my limited energy talking.

But however hard we swam, the castle just wasn't getting closer.

'Where's the tunnel?' Shona asked.

I shook my head. 'No good,' I said. 'Can't hold my breath. Have to go this way.'

I tried to do what I'd done the first time the ring had led me to the tunnel. Tried to let go, listen to the ring. I stroked the gold band as we swam and twisted the ring round so I could see the diamond sparkle and glint on my finger.

It was leading us there. I could feel it, even if I couldn't swim through the tunnel, even if the current was so slight I could have imagined it, even if the castle only seemed to be getting closer a millimetre at a time. We were still getting there, and the ring was doing all it could to help. Maybe it was getting weaker, like me.

Please hold out, I begged silently. *Please get us there.*

We seemed to have been swimming forever.

'I can't do it,' I cried. Tears were starting to slip down my face. 'I can't do it.'

'Emily, look!' Shona let go of my hand to point ahead. I followed the line of her finger. 'The castle!' she said. 'We're getting closer!'

She was right. In the half light, I could see it more clearly than ever. The mist lay across its middle like a belt. Above, three large turrets stood proud, serrated against the deep blue night. Its windows shone as though polished, black and dark, hiding a thousand secrets behind them.

Below the mist, rocks were emerging by the second. Huge boulders lay dotted about on the stony beach. In between them, jagged rocks were scattered everywhere, like a range of forbidding mountains. Waves thundered against them.

The sight of the castle so close spurred me on. I tried flicking my tail, but it hardly moved. My arms were weakening with every stroke, my tail growing more and more like a plank of heavy wood with every flick.

And then the moon began to rise.

First the tip, poking out through the sea, growing bigger with every moment, until it was whole. The most enormous orange ball, balancing on the water, it slowly edged its way into the sky. We'd have maybe twenty or thirty minutes till it had fully risen. It wasn't long enough.

'We're never going to do it,' I said. 'We might as well give up.'

But before Shona had a chance to reply, a voice called across to us in the darkness. 'Emily!'

I peered ahead, scanning the rocks.

'There!' Shona screeched, jabbing a finger at one of the huge jagged rocks, sharp and pointed as a witch's hat, and just as black. A figure stood halfway up its side. Aaron!

'Emily! Hurry!' he called. 'Please hurry!'

I couldn't give up! Of *course* I couldn't. It didn't matter if every single cell in my body wanted to scream with exhaustion. I had to get there.

Shona held tightly on to my hand. 'We can do it,' she said, again and again. 'I'm going to get you there.' But pulling a dead weight along in the water can't be easy for anyone, and even Shona was starting to get tired. Still the castle lay out of reach. *Come on, come on, we have to get there.* Inwardly, I urged myself on, screamed instructions and demands, begged, bribed. *Just get there. I'll do anything.*

The moon climbed slowly upwards, growing fatter and whiter by the second. Any moment, the curse would be complete and it would all be over. Neptune would be here to claim his ring – and he'd be bringing my parents to say goodbye. My chances of solving all this would be lost forever, along with everything I cared about.

165

I splashed through the water, clumsy and awkward like a puppy in a lake. Useless. Useless! The castle seemed to be getting further away. The moon shone down, its beam like a searchlight across the top of the ocean. I kept my eyes on the water ahead of me, hiding from the shaft of light like a fugitive. If it didn't catch me, maybe we were safe.

I glanced up at the castle. Still too far away. It looked like a cardboard cut-out against the night sky. A dark silhouette, the little figure of Aaron standing on the rocks, waving and calling to us. His voice seemed to be getting fainter.

And then something else.

As I stared, a thick black cloud came from nowhere, swirling like a shoal of black fish, then spreading out, slinking like a snake; twisting, turning up, down, circling round and round. It looked like a giant swarm of bees.

They moved as one, towards me and Shona. As they did, I saw what it was: birds. Instantly, they flicked and turned, back towards the castle. In a private dance for us, they wove with perfect grace and timing around and around the castle, gliding in slow motion, as though silently sliding down the banister of a spiral staircase; then bunching into a black ball again, spinning above the castle.

The dance went on and on as the birds whirled upwards in the shape of a genie emerging from his lamp. Then, as one, they spread out and flew towards us in a fan. An enormous flock of tiny black birds passed over our heads, chattering in a million different languages and briefly turning the sky black before they disappeared into the distance.

Seconds later, they were back, coming towards us again: more of them this time, a thick black line of them dividing the sky. They just kept coming and coming, more and more of them, to dance and swirl and break up and re-form around the castle.

'What in the ocean is that?' Shona said eventually, her voice breathless and tight.

'The starlings!' I said.

'Starlings? Are you sure?' Shona asked.

'Positive.'

'But starlings don't fly at night, do they? And certainly not out in the middle of the ocean.'

I shook my head. 'Look at the sky, Shona.' It was brightening by the second as the moon climbed higher and higher. 'This is no ordinary night.'

'You can say that again,' Shona breathed. 'What are they doing though?'

As if to answer her, the birds formed themselves into a tight, perfect cone. Pointed and sharp at its base, it twisted and whirled towards the rocks, round and round like an electric drill. Hovering over a bunch of rocks right at the water's edge, the cone spun as though boring into the ground. As it did, the ring burned on my finger, heating my hand, filling my body with warmth and emotion. And in that moment, I knew.

I turned to Shona. 'They're helping us,' I said. 'They want us to find the ring.'

They must have done it every year. They were connected to the ring, somehow, and Aaron's great-grandfather had figured out that much, too. But we had more on our side than he'd had. We had the ring. And we had the moon. I glanced up. Higher and higher it climbed.

Suddenly I wasn't tired any longer. 'The starlings!' I screamed into the air, jumping to life as though I'd been struck by lightning. 'Aaron! Follow the starlings!' That's what the paintings had been telling us. I had no doubts at all now. I pointed at the sky, jabbing my fingers again and again at the birds.

Aaron stared at the black swarm above his head. Then, as though the same flash of lightning had struck him too, he juddered into action. Clambering down the rock, he raced to the edge of the water and fell to his knees, scrabbling in the sand and round the rocks.

The moon edged up another notch, shining so strongly the sky lightened as it rose. It was almost like daylight. It was nearly there! *Please Aaron, find it, find it.* I watched him scrape at the water's edge, stopping to look up at the starlings, then back to the ground, a new spot, a different position, lifting rocks, tossing them aside, digging into the stony ground. Every time, his hands came back empty.

As we swam on, the water seemed to turn against us. Waves came from nowhere, splashing our faces, ducking me under. Eddies broke out around us. Small whirlpools. Bubbles cracking and popping like lava. What was happening?

Shona caught my eye. 'It's Neptune,' she said, her face white and thin. 'He must be on his way.'

'Emily!' Aaron screamed to us. He was waving his hands in the air. 'Look!' He pointed just below the base of the starlings' cone. It was too far away to see exactly what he was pointing at but as the moon edged even higher, I saw something glint and sparkle, just below the rocks he was standing on. As the sea withdrew even further, it shone brighter. The ring.

We'd found the ring! We'd really done it! The starlings swarmed around the rocks, their wings purple and green against the bright moonlight, before they separated, the line thinning out as they started to move away. Their job was done.

A spurt of energy drove me on. I had to get there before Neptune. Before the moon had fully risen. Before the curse was over and it was all too late. Urgent thoughts whipped at my mind like the waves whipped across my face, lashing me, crashing against each other like cymbals. *No, they won't beat me. They won't. We've got the rings. We can do it.* Over and over, I repeated the same words.

'Hurry, Emily!' Aaron called as he stepped towards the ring.

And then, an enormous wave came from nowhere, washing over me, hurling me down into the sea where I could no longer swim. I pounded back up to the surface, gasping for air.

As soon as I caught my breath, I scanned the rocks. Huge frothy waves engulfed the spot where Aaron had been standing only moments earlier.

There was no sign of him.

Where was he? What had happened to him?

'Emily!' Shona called me. She'd been thrown even further away from me. 'Hang on! I'll get you,' she cried.

Another set of waves threw me under almost immediately, dunking me again and again, only just giving me time to catch the smallest breath in between.

I couldn't keep fighting against it. I wasn't going to get there. So near, so near. But it was impossible. I wasn't going to make it.

I cried with all the energy I had left, my tears adding the smallest salty drops into the raging ocean. I stopped trying to swim, stopped trying to fight. 'You win!' I screamed at the sky, the moon, at the sea. 'I give up!'

It was all over. I'd lost everything. My one

chance to keep my parents together and carry on living with them both. My life as a semi-mer – all of it gone, taking Aaron's future with it too.

Chapter Thirteen

As I cried, I looked hopelessly out at the sea all around me. We'd never get out of this alive. Shona had drifted further away. She was still calling me. 'I'll get to you. Just hang on,' she cried.

But I could hardly keep my head above the water. When the waves weren't crashing over my head, I was sinking down into huge swells, rising up only to be thrown under again.

Then I slipped down into the biggest swell yet. All I could see on every side of me was a deep blue wall of water. It was like a well, with me at the bottom. Surely this was it. I opened my mouth to pray for my life.

But the wave didn't break. As it washed past me, I rose up on to another crest. I searched the skyline for Shona. Nothing. Where was she? I craned my neck, squinting into the distance.

I scrutinised every wave, all the way to the castle, searched every rock. And then I saw it. A boat. A small, green, abandoned rowing boat, paint peeling from it everywhere, its wood rotting and half burnt.

The thought crashed into my head as hard as the waves. The boat could save us. If only Shona could somehow get it to me. Where was she? I searched the horizon. There! I saw her head! We could do this!

'Emily!' Shona called again.

'The boat! Get the boat!' I cried. My voice was hoarse, screaming over thunderous waves.

'I can't hear you!' Shona yelled back. She was swimming back to me. A wave engulfed me before I could reply.

Gasping, pulling hair off my forehead and choking back sea water in my throat, I called back to her. 'The boat!' I cried. 'There's a boat. Find Aaron. Get him in the boat.' Another wave hit me. I choked as I swallowed a mouthful of salty water.

Shona searched the rocky beach. 'That?' she asked, pointing to the abandoned rowing boat. It was half filled with water.

I nodded. 'Just do it. It's our only hope. Quickly!'

Shona gripped my hand for a second. 'Stay here, Emily. Just stay here. You'll be fine. I'll come back for you. OK?' Her voice broke as she looked at me.

'Go,' I said. 'Hurry.'

Shona turned and swam away from me, zooming off at full speed towards the rocky beach, the abandoned boat, the boy I hoped with all my heart was still there somewhere.

I watched the moon climb ever higher. How much time did we have? Minutes? Would she find him? Did he have the ring? My head was ready to burst with questions.

I squinted across at the castle, the rocky beach. She'd made it! Shona was at the water's edge, dragging the boat into the water. Please find Aaron. Please find him.

'Emily!'

Someone was calling me. Near the rocks.

'Someone! Help me!'

Aaron! I could just see his head bobbing on the waves, his hand high in the air, curled into a fist. 'I've got it! I've got it!' he shouted. 'Someone help me!'

'Shona!' I yelled with every bit of energy I could muster. She was edging the boat from the shore. I pointed desperately to Aaron. As she turned to look, he waved his fist again. Instantly, Shona pushed the boat out, swimming across towards him. As she pulled alongside him, he clambered over the side, practically falling into the boat.

Come on, come on. All I could do now was wait here, and hope with all my might that they got here before the moon had fully risen. I looked up. Surely it was nearly there. *Hurry!*

Shona was behind the boat, pushing it along, her tail spinning furiously as the boat dipped and rolled with the waves. It kept disappearing out of sight as huge swells moved across it, rolling towards me. Each time it happened, I held my breath, closed my eyes and prayed that it would appear over the top of the next crest. And each time, thank goodness, it did.

Closer and closer, the boat edged towards me, Shona swimming, propelling it along, her tail its only engine, Aaron sitting up in the boat, one hand raised aloft in a fist. The ring was inside his fist, I knew it. *Please!* I begged silently for them to reach me soon; my body was weakening with every second. My tail had all but disappeared now. My legs felt as though they were glued together and numb. Only my feet were replaced with the tip of my tail.

My breathing scratched and tore at my lungs. I couldn't hold on much longer.

'Emily!' Shona called as I flailed about, desperately trying to stay afloat. They were here!

'You were right!' Aaron called as they edged

closer. 'The starlings, they pointed right at it. All these years I've seen them. I never knew. We never knew.' He leaned out of the boat as they glided towards me. 'Grab my hand.'

I swam towards them, as fast as I could, reaching up with my hand, holding it as high out of the water as I could. We were really going to do it! I smiled as my eyes met Aaron's. His fingers were centimetres from mine.

And then it hit me. The biggest wave of the lot. Smashing over my head, almost knocking me out, throwing me down, deep under the water, flipping the boat into the air. All I could see was a fountain of froth and bubbles, and sand swirling all around me. I swallowed about a gallon of water; my lungs were on fire.

Pushing with all the strength I had left, I kicked with what remained of my tail, clutching at water with my hands as though I could claw my way through it. Eventually, I made it back to the surface. Coughing and spluttering, I knew that was the last time I could do that. Next time I would have no strength left to pull myself up.

'Aaron,' I gasped. 'Shona!'

They were nowhere to be seen.

And then the sea really erupted, shaking and rocking like the biggest whirlpool in the world. I knew it could only mean one thing: Neptune had arrived.

I saw him in the distance, his chariot pulled swiftly along by about twenty dolphins. They charged towards us. I felt like a prisoner on death row, ready to give up completely.

'Emily!' A voice called behind me. I swivelled round. Aaron! One hand still held high in the air, he was paddling towards me on a piece of driftwood. 'The boat collapsed,' he gasped. 'This is all that's left.'

I swam frantically towards him, willing my tail to hold out just a few more moments.

'The moon,' Aaron panted. 'We've only got a minute.'

A wave washed over my head, but I shook it off. Paddling furiously, I made it to the makeshift raft and grabbed hold of it, gasping for breath. One more minute and then I'd lose the ring forever. Everything that mattered to me would slip down to the bottom of the sea with it, never to be seen again.

I could hear Neptune roaring instructions at the dolphins, waving his trident in the air.

'Now!' I said, holding my hand out. Aaron was wearing the other ring. He held his hand out to mine. The pearl glowed white. The diamond burst with brightness. It was almost blinding. The sea bubbled and boiled all around us as we fumbled to try and bring the two rings together. Come on, come *on*!

Neptune was in front of us, his face as angry as the darkest thunderstorm, his trident high above his head, his eyes burning with rage, his mouth open to shout at us. And then –

The sea stopped moving.

The mist cleared.

Neptune opened his mouth to yell at us. Our hands met.

And the rings came together.

Chapter Fourteen

We'd done it! We'd really, truly done it.

We held the rings between us, each gripping the raft with the other hand. Light fizzed out from them like an exploding box of fireworks. White lights rocketing to the sky, bright blue balls of energy whizzing round and round, orange bubbles exploding all around us. I laughed with relief, tears rolling down my cheeks.

With every spark, I felt the life return to my broken body. My tail burst into action with the light, filling up, flicking the water. My tail had come back! I was still a semi-mer! We'd beaten the curse!

'Look!' Aaron arched his body; something flipped on to the water behind him. A tail! Sleek and black, it shone and glowed as it batted the surface of the sea. 'My tail,' he said, staring at it in wonder. 'I've got a tail!'

'We did it!' I cried, clenching his hand tight as we held the two rings together.

And then Neptune rose in his chariot, his figure blocking out the moon itself.

He opened his mouth to speak, to roar, to do all the things Neptune does. I squeezed my eyes shut in anticipation. What would he say? What would he do now? Surely he wasn't going to leave it like this. How could we have thought for the tiniest second that we could get away with it?

But no sound came. Eventually, I opened my eyes again, to see Neptune in the same position; his hand in the air, his body taut and tense, the sea around him motionless. He was staring in our direction, but not at us.

I turned to see what he was looking at. At first I thought it was just the mist, hovering around the castle as it always did, bunching up into a ball. But there was something inside the mist. A person. A woman. She had the most beautiful face I'd ever seen. Eyes as green as the brightest emeralds, framed by thick black lashes. Her hair was jet-black, stretching down her back. She reached out a hand to Neptune, holding his eyes with hers.

'Aurora?' he said eventually. 'Is that really you?'

Aurora? The woman who broke Neptune's heart?

As she smiled back at him, her eyes brightened even more. Her smile seemed to lighten the whole ocean. 'It's really me.'

'How? How are you here?' Neptune's voice grew harder. 'Is it magic? A trick of the light? What is it? How do you come before me like this?'

'Every year at the spring equinox, I wait for you. I try to find you. I have never seen you until this time . . . ' She swept a hand in front of us, smiling down at me and Aaron as she did so. It felt like the sun coming out. 'This time, the rings have come back together, and they have brought me to you, and you to me.'

'But you left me,' Neptune replied, his voice hardening. 'You broke my heart. You cannot mend it. You can never undo the suffering you caused me!'

Aurora held a slender finger to her mouth. 'Don't say this. Never say such a thing. I would never leave you.'

'Liar! You did. You left me!'

'I was a mortal. I wished with all my heart not to be. I even tried. For you. And I drowned, trying to swim to you . . . '

Her voice was fading. The mist swirled around

her face, wrapping around her like a scarf. 'You must forgive me,' she whispered.

'Aurora!' Neptune called. Waving his trident at the sky, he cried. 'Don't go! I ORDER you to stay! Do NOT leave me!'

The mist had all but swept her away. Her image. Her spirit. Whatever it was, it had almost faded completely.

'It's gone midnight. The moon has passed its fullness. We are moving into day, towards the light, the spring, new life. I cannot stay. Forgive me,' she said, her voice as gentle as a breeze. 'Forgive me. I beg you, forgive me.' Again and again, she repeated the same words, until there was no more voice, no vision, only the wind and the moon and the night.

In the silence, we watched the mist that continued to swirl around the castle, wrapping it in fog. Neptune stared the hardest. His eyes didn't flicker.

Aaron let go of my hand. 'Look,' he whispered. Under the moon's power, the pull of the rings had loosened. Aaron slipped his from his finger. Putting it carefully on the raft, he held his hands up. In the moonlight, I suddenly realised what he was looking at. The webbing. It had gone.

Gently placing my ring next to his, I examined my own hands. They'd gone back to normal too! I laughed with pleasure, grinning at Aaron, at Shona, at —

'Gotcha!' A hand snapped up out of nowhere,

snatching the rings from the raft.

'No!' I lunged forward to grab them back, but it was too late. I dived down into the water. Fuelled with new energy, my mermaid self intact, I swam as hard as I could to catch whoever it was who had stolen the rings. But he was too fast for me. He bolted away, swimming like a lightning streak towards Neptune's chariot.

When I came back up to the surface, I saw who it was. Smiling his smarmy, creepy, nasty smile, holding out the rings for Neptune to take. Who else?

Mr Beeston.

'Neptune won't fall for any of that sentimental codswallop!' he snarled. 'Oh no, he knows what is important in life. What really matters, what – '

'Beeston!' Neptune growled.

Mr Beeston bowed low, holding the rings out in front of him as he flicked his tail to tread water. 'Your Majesty,' he said, his voice deep and intense. 'I humbly return to you what is rightfully yours. I swore my allegiance to you and I have not failed you. Finally, the rings are back with you. Once again, they may be parted and buried, safely out of trouble. And you have my word, I will never, ever let anything like this happen again.' Mr Beeston carried on bowing so low his head was practically underwater. No one else moved. No one spoke.

Then Neptune held out a hand. 'Give me the

rings,' he said.

Mr Beeston instantly swam forward to hand the rings over to Neptune. 'Your Majesty, I am humbled by your – '

'Silence!' Neptune barked, his face contorted – with rage, with pain? I couldn't tell.

I stared at him. After everything we'd done, everything that had happened, how could it go wrong so quickly? Now Neptune had the rings back, he could curse us all over again – and this time there wouldn't be a single thing we could do about it.

I sank lower in the water, my tail hardly moving. Shona swam over to join me. She took hold of my hand. 'I'll always be your best friend,' she whispered. 'Whatever happens.'

But maybe she wouldn't have that choice. None of us had any choices any more. All the choices were in Neptune's hands. Literally.

Neptune flicked his trident in the air. Instantly, three dolphins swam to the side of the chariot. He bent down to say something to them and they disappeared, returning moments later pulling something along. Another chariot, a sleigh of some kind. There were two people in it. A woman and – a merman. No! It couldn't be! But it was! Mum and Dad! Of course! Neptune said he'd bring them tonight!

I swam as hard as I could to reach the boat.

'Mum! Dad!' I cried with every tiny bit of me. But the joy I felt disappeared as soon as I saw their faces.

Of course.

They had come to say goodbye.

Here, under the full moon, on the spring equinox, the one point in the year when day meets night, earth and sea would finally be separated, and for good this time.

Mum reached out from the carriage to throw her arms round me. 'Oh Emily,' she sobbed, grasping my hair, pulling me to her so tightly I couldn't breathe. I didn't care. All that mattered was that I was in my mother's arms again. 'I looked for you everywhere. Everyone on the island has been searching. We found every last jewel that Neptune had been after, but we couldn't find the most precious one of all. You.'

Then Dad's arms were round me too. Hovering in the water next to me, he reached out to wrap me in his arms. 'My little 'un,' he said, his voice raw and broken.

'Windsnap!' Neptune bellowed. All three of us looked up at him. He was pointing at Dad. 'Come here,' he said firmly.

Dad let go of me.

'No!' I lurched on to him, gripping him round the neck with my arms. This was it. My dad was going to be taken away; I'd say goodbye to him for the last time. 'No! Please!' I begged.

Dad unpeeled my fingers from around his neck. 'It'll be OK,' he said, the quivering in his voice giving him away. He didn't believe that any more than I did. Then he looked Mum in the eye. 'I always loved you,' he said. 'And I always will, right?'

Mum swallowed hard and nodded.

Dad glanced at Neptune, who glared back at him. 'I have to go,' he said. Kissing Mum's hand, ruffling my hair, he turned and swam away.

I darted through the water to follow him. Gripping his arm, I swam alongside him. Dad tried to shake me off. 'Please, little 'un, don't make this harder than it already is,' he said.

'Don't go,' I begged. I swam to Neptune's chariot with him. 'Please!' I begged Neptune, choking on sobs. 'Please don't make me have to lose my dad again. Please. Please don't make them have to part. I'll do anything. I'll be good. I'll never get into trouble again. *Please.*' I let go of Dad and wept openly. I had nothing left to say, nothing to ask, nothing to offer, nothing to look forward to.

'Stop your crying, child,' said Neptune. 'Listen to me.' He turned to Dad, looking him harshly in the eyes. 'Windsnap,' he said. 'Do you love your wife?'

'More than anything,' Dad said. He looked round for inspiration – and found it in the sky. 'More than the moon itself.'

Nodding briskly, Neptune asked, 'And she feels the same way?'

Dad glanced across at Mum. 'I hope so.'

Mum held her hands to her chest. Wiping her cheeks with the back of her hand, she nodded vigorously.

Neptune was silent for a long time. He put his trident down on the seat in his chariot and held the rings in both hands. Juggling them in his palms, he looked back and forth between Mum and Dad. His powerful face looked different. The lines of anger streaking down each cheek seemed to have gone. His eyes looked rounder, softer. For the first time ever, I noticed how green they were.

In the darkness, rain began to fall, tiny sharp droplets plopping onto the sea all around us. Neptune opened his mouth to speak again.

'No one has to say goodbye tonight,' he said quietly. He turned to Mr Beeston. 'Beeston,' he said. 'You were wrong.'

Mr Beeston swam forward. Bowing low so his hair fell right into the water, he gabbled, 'Your Majesty, if I have failed you in any way, I – '

Neptune raised a hand to silence him. 'You acted out of loyalty. But you are mistaken. I do not know what is important in life, what really matters. Or if I do, I have only just found out.' He looked up at the mist, still swirling around the castle. The rain fell harder, bouncing off the sea all around us. 'I have only just remembered.'

Then he held the rings out in front of him. 'Come here, Windsnap,' he said. Picking up his trident, he nodded to the dolphins, who instantly swam forward, bringing the carriage and Mum to Neptune.

What was he doing? 'I will no longer hide from the truth. I will no longer attempt to bury my feelings,' he said.

Neptune called Aaron. 'You are the man of the family now,' he said to Aaron. 'I cannot undo what has been done. But I can make amends. You are free to travel, to live where you please, mix with whoever you like. I will not hide you from the world any longer. You are my fin and blood and I am proud of you.'

Aaron smiled hesitantly at Neptune. His eyes, his deep green eyes. Neptune's eyes.

'Your Majesty, sir,' he said. 'What about my mother?'

'She will be waiting for you at the castle.'

'Is she . . . ?'

Neptune nodded. 'She will be fine,' he said. 'Like

you, she has a long life ahead of her. I want you both to enjoy it.'

'You mean she's better? We're no longer cursed?' Aaron burst out.

Laughing, Neptune replied, 'I will no longer allow curses. They are forbidden – by law!'

Aaron punched the air. Then he turned and smiled the widest smile at me.

Neptune turned back to my parents. 'I am a firm ruler,' he said. 'And I always will be. No one can ever try to deny this.' Mum and Dad both nodded, waiting for him to continue.

'But,' Neptune went on, beckoning me to come to him. 'But this daughter of yours has brought something back to me which I lost many hundreds of years ago.' He fell silent.

'The rings?' I asked, hoping to prompt him, even though I should have known better than to interrupt Neptune.

'No,' he said gently. 'Not the rings. You and your family may never fully understand what you have given me, but let me tell you, it is the most valuable thing. In return, I give it back to you.' Then he reached out to Mum and Dad – and handed them the rings! The diamond one to Dad, the pearl to Mum.

Silently receiving the rings, Mum and Dad gazed at each other, at me, at Neptune.

'You represent what I have lost, and you will

represent its revival too.' He spread his arms upwards to the sky. 'It is the spring equinox,' he called, 'the day of my wedding anniversary, the day of new beginnings. Merfolk and humans will from now on live in peace together. I order it!'

I gasped and looked at Shona. Really? Did he really say that?

'Not just on one small island. It's time for the whole world to start again. We will start a new world. A new world that is not a new world at all. The world that was there all along, to anyone who was not too blind to see it.'

Then he turned back to us and frowned. 'But you must make me a promise,' he said sternly. I *knew* there'd be a catch. I knew it couldn't be that simple. Nothing in my life ever was.

'You must swear to me that these rings will never again be parted.'

Dad grinned so widely his smile almost broke his face in two. Grabbing Mum round the waist and pulling me towards him with his other arm, he replied, 'Your Majesty, that is the easiest of promises to keep.'

Neptune smiled. 'Very well. I have said all I need to say.' Holding his trident in the air, he waved it in the direction of *Fortuna*. A group of dolphins broke away and swam off towards it. 'Your boat will be fit to sail by morning,' Neptune said. 'Now go. Travel the world. See new sights. Pass the message on to all you meet.'

'We will,' Mum breathed. 'We won't let you down, your Majesty. How can we ever thank you?'

Neptune waved her words away with his hand. 'Just respect the rings and what they represent. I am giving you a great responsibility. You must show me you are ready for this. I shall be watching you.'

With that, Neptune clicked his fingers and held his trident aloft. Motioning for Mr Beeston to join him, he sat back down in his chariot.

'Look, I never meant you any harm,' Mr Beeston mumbled as he passed. Blushing and stammering, he added, 'I didn't mean to – you know. It was just duty, you understand. Loyalty. I mean, Neptune. He's the king. We're still friends, aren't we?'

'Friends?' Mum spluttered. 'When have we ever been real friends?'

Dad touched her gently on the arm. 'Penny,' he said. 'It's a new world. We have to set an example.'

Penny. He called her Penny! Things really were back to normal. Better than normal!

'Just like that?' asked Mum. 'After everything?'

Dad nodded. 'Look at all we have to be grateful for. Let's start again.'

Mum turned to Mr Beeston.

'Very well,' Mum sighed. 'We'll try. But as long as you remember you have to be loyal to us too, now.'

'I will,' Mr Beeston simpered. 'I will. Thank you. Thank you.' Then he gave me one last lopsided smile. 'No hard feelings, eh?' he said, reaching out to ruffle my hair.

I stiffened, dodging his hand. 'Mm,' I said. I wasn't ready to forgive and forget yet.

'Emily,' Dad said firmly.

'OK. Whatever.'

And then the strangest thing happened. We looked at each other, me and Mr Beeston. And for the first time in my life, I felt that we really saw each other; saw, heard and understood each other. I saw someone like me. Desperate to fit in, to please, to belong. That was all he wanted. And when he smiled at me, I didn't recoil and squirm and think about his crooked teeth and his odd eyes. I found myself smiling back. 'Yeah,' I said. 'No hard feelings.'

'That's a good girl,' he said.

'Beeston!' Neptune called again and Mr Beeston swam off to join him in his chariot. As the dolphins pulled them away, the moonlight lit a trail ahead of them.

In the silence of the night, I could hear Neptune's voice as they sailed away. 'I forgive you,' he called to the sky. 'I forgive you.'

As his words echoed through the dark night, Dad pointed up into the sky. 'Look at that,' he said. I wouldn't have thought it possible if I hadn't seen it with my own eyes. The moonlight sparkled on the sea, lighting up the raindrops that kept falling. In the distance, the castle stood dark and solid. But the mist had completely cleared. In its place, framing it with a perfect arc, every colour bright and clear, was a rainbow.

'Just go through it once more,' Millie said, blinking round at us all on the front deck. Aaron's mum was sitting on the front benches with her and Mum. She looked just like Aaron, thin and pale with jet-black hair. She hadn't said much since she'd joined us, but she'd smiled a lot. A great wide smile that infected everyone around her, just like Aaron's.

Dad leaned over a rail along the side of the boat. Aaron was in the water with me and Shona.

The sky was pale blue, wispy clouds floating lazily across it, each one tinged with pink edges. Millie had only just woken up. None of the rest of us had been asleep at all. How could we have slept on a night like this?

Mum laughed as she handed Millie a cup of tea. 'We've told you the story three times now!'

'Yes, but I still don't believe it!' Millie replied, closing her eyes in ecstasy as she sipped her tea.

'Nor do we,' Dad said, smiling at Mum as he reached for her hand. The rings shone on their fingers. 'But it's true.'

Millie took another gulp from her cup.

'We can go anywhere we like,' Mum said. 'We don't need to hide what we are.' Then she glanced at Shona. 'Of course, we'll go back to Allpoints Island first. These last few days I've realised how much everyone there cares about us. We may even stay there for good if we want to.'

'Swishy!' Shona and I shouted in unison.

'Can we go too, Mother?' Aaron asked.

'I don't see why not,' his mum replied with a laugh.

'Of course you're coming too,' Mum said, linking her arm. 'We're not letting you go that easily.'

'And if we ever get bored with Allpoints Island, we'll move somewhere else. Anywhere we like,' Dad said, his eyes shining with excitement.

'And if we don't, we'll just take lots of holidays,' Mum smiled.

'We'll visit every country, every land, every sea,' Dad went on. 'We'll show the whole world they can get on in harmony like us!'

'We will, darling,' Mum said, smiling back at him. 'And maybe we'll even bring a tutor along with us so Emily doesn't miss out on her schooling.'

'Perfect!' Dad said. 'She'll come back from her travels and still get top marks in Shipwrecks and Sand Dunes.'

Mum's face tightened. 'I was thinking more of

her sums and spellings, Jake.'

'I'll get her a new hairbrush, a whole set of hairbrushes, and an ocean chart so she can recognise all the fish in the sea.'

'Or a ruler and a dictionary,' Mum insisted.

'Oh, you two,' Millie sighed. 'You're not at it again, are you?'

Mum and Dad looked at each other and burst out laughing. 'OK,' Dad said. 'Maybe changing the world is a bit ambitious just now.'

'We'll start small,' Mum said, reaching for his hand.

Dad kissed her palm. 'Lead by example,' he said. 'No arguing.'

'Never,' Mum agreed.

'Come on,' I said. 'Let's get going. Shona needs to get back to her parents!'

We'd hooked *Fortuna* up to some ropes so we could tow it back. I don't know what Neptune had done, but the lower deck was dry and sealed up so it floated like a normal boat. 'We'll put it back to normal when we get home,' Dad smiled.

With a bit of help from Aaron's maps, we'd set a course back to Allpoints Island. Dad reckoned it would only take a few days if we took turns at pulling. He had left it to the three of us for now while he hitched on to the side of the boat near Mum.

Shona and Aaron and I pulled on the ropes as we

set off, flipping our tails to make rainbows with the water, ducking under to see the rubbery round yellow fish with big black eyes bouncing on the seabed, racing and chasing each other all the way.

As we passed the castle, we fell silent. Without the mist, it looked almost naked. Lonely, even. 'We'll come back,' Aaron's mother called down. 'Even if it's just for a visit.'

Aaron smiled up at her, then splashed me and grinned. He pulled his rope taut. 'Race you to the next wave!' he said with a grin.

Shona dived down to follow him. But I stayed close to the boat for a while. The sky was growing lighter and lighter. Up behind me I could hear Mum and Dad talking.

'I've nothing against rulers,' Dad was saying. 'But protractors. I mean, come on, does she really need one of those?'

'I tell you what,' Mum replied. 'I'll let you have the scale polish if you give me the algebra set.'

'The scale polish and a kiss,' Dad said.

'Done.'

They were quiet for a while after that.

I smiled to myself as we swam on. What lay ahead for us? Where would we go? What would the future hold?

I couldn't answer the questions spinning round in my head any more than I could stop Mum and Dad bickering about my schooling, or Shona worrying about her hair, or Millie trying to tell fortunes with coat-hangers.

It didn't matter. What mattered was what I could see around me: my best friend racing our new friend along the surf; Mum and Dad smiling at each other and joking and kissing; Millie spreading the tarot cards out on the deck for Aaron's mum.

And beyond that? Well, beyond that lay a brand new day.

Behind the scenes of the

Windsnap World

with Radio Merwave

Ladies and gentlemen, merfolk and merkids, Radio Merwave is delighted to bring you the third in our series of exclusive behind-the-scenes interviews with some of your favourite characters. I'm Simon Watermark and today I'm talking to Aaron Halflight.

Simon: Aaron, thank you for joining us.

Aaron: Thank you for having me.

Simon: I've interviewed a lot of merfolk over the years, but, I have to say, I was particularly looking forward to interviewing you.

Aaron: Why's that?

Simon: Your story fascinates me. Your background – it's so different from anyone else's.

Aaron: (Laughs.) Yes, I suppose it probably is.

Simon: I'm sure our readers would love to hear more. So how about talking us through a typical day in the life of Halflight Castle?

Aaron: I don't know if there is such a thing as a typical day. I mean, I suppose the days have all been quite similar recently – but they're very different from when I was younger. Which do you want to hear about?

Simon: Both! How about we start with life when you were little?

Aaron: Well, there were a lot more folk around. For a start, there was my father . . .

Simon: Tell us about your father.

Aaron: He was proud, hard-working, strict. And loyal. There was nothing he wouldn't do for his family. (Pause.) Even die for us.

Simon: Yes, I heard about that. We're all terribly sorry.

Aaron: Thank you.

Simon: Would you rather I ask about something different?

Aaron: (Pause.) No, it's OK. It's nice to talk about him.

Simon: Please tell us more then . . .

Aaron: Well, he taught me lots of things.

Simon: Like what?

Aaron: How to swim – which was pretty useful as it's not easy when you're stuck with a curse that means you have neither a proper tail, nor fully formed feet.

Simon: Hmm, I can see that might be a problem.

Aaron: Not for my father, it wasn't. He took me out every day, whatever the weather – when the sea was flat calm or when the white horses were racing across jagged waves and rearing up over the rocks. He'd go ahead and make me swim through tunnels and around the currents to reach him. He gave me loads of confidence – both in the water and out of it.

Simon: He sounds like a great father.

Aaron: He was. The best. When I was about six, he taught me to catch fish on a line. He told me that one day I would be the man of the house and that he wanted to pass on all his skills while he was still around to do so. It's because of him that I've learned to look after myself the way I have. He made me strong and independent.

Simon: So you learned to swim and to fish. What about learning other things? Did you go to school?

Aaron: I've lived in Halflight Castle all my life,

cut off from everywhere – there was no school in that world.

Simon: And yet you seem to be such an educated young chap. Where did it all come from?

Aaron: Books, maps, charts – the products of many years of wrecks and pirate hauls that came our way.

Simon: Who taught you, or did you just work your way through it all yourself?

Aaron: Bits of it I did myself. Mostly it was the sirens, though. There were always a few installed in the sea around the castle. Halflight has always relied on them to keep the ships and their produce coming our way.

Simon: And they educated you?

Aaron: (Laughs.) Don't sound so surprised.

Simon: It's not exactly how most folk view sirens.

Aaron: Most folk don't know the half of it. They were always good to me and my family. Brought us the good, kept away the bad – and made sure I stuck with my studies in between.

Simon: So what

happened to the sirens?

Aaron: They stopped coming, like everyone else. We used to have lots of visitors – the regular pirates, the captains of ships who the sirens chose to befriend rather than wreck on our rocks. There was always laughter at the castle when I was little, and always lots of fun.

Simon: Sounds great.

Aaron: It was. Sometimes, the sirens would lure a ship to us, but instead of leading it to crash on the rocks, they'd invite the crew to live with us for a while – on the condition that they shared some of their food and left us some of their wares. I loved it when that happened. The castle would be full of life – parties every night.

Simon: Was there singing?

Aaron: Are you kidding? With a castle full of sirens and sailors? There was singing till dawn! Dancing, too. A captain's wife once spent three days teaching me the foxtrot. I can't wait to dance again, now my feet aren't like big floppy paddles!

Simon: How long would this go on for?

Aaron: Sometimes a few nights, sometimes weeks. They'd always leave us with a few

valuables to trade with
the next ship. I loved
those days.

Simon: So what happened?
Why did they end?

Aaron: Neptune got to hear about
the friendships, and he wasn't impressed.
He banished them all.

Simon: No more friendly pirates?

Aaron: No more friendly anything.

Simon: Sounds terrible. So can I ask about your
more recent days at Halflight Castle, or is it too
painful?

Aaron: It has been really painful. After father …
and then mother being so ill. These last few
months have been really hard. There are days
when I think I can't bear it, and then I hear
my father's voice in my head, urging me on.

Simon: Like when he was teaching you to swim?

Aaron: Exactly! I can hear him telling me, 'Go
on, son, you can do it'. That's the only thing
that's given me the strength to get through a
lot of the days recently.

Simon: You're an incredible young merman,
Aaron. Very inspiring. And now, of course, things
have all changed again.

Aaron: You mean because of the curse being lifted?

Simon: Absolutely! How does that feel?

Aaron: It feels incredible. Mother is healthy again. She's even smiled a few times in the last couple of days. And look at my tail!

Simon: Errr, you do remember that this is radio, don't you?

Aaron: (Laughs.) Sorry, well my tail's never properly formed until this week. Nor have my feet. And the fact that I can now go from one to the other when I go in and out of the water – I just can't tell you how amazing that is.

Simon: Aaron, you're an inspiration. I really wish you all the best with your future.

Aaron: Thank you.

Simon: Now, before we go, let's have some quick-fire questions.

Aaron: OK.

Simon: What's your favourite hobby?

Aaron: Map reading! I know it sounds a bit dull, but it isn't. I just love poring over maps and plotting the routes of the ships that have visited us, and making up stories for where they might have gone next.

Simon: That doesn't sound dull at all! How about your favourite colour?

Aaron: **Black. I like it because it's a colour you can hide behind. Also, I love my black hair – I think it makes me look more cool and mysterious than I really am!**

Simon: How about your favourite person?

Aaron: **(Pause.)**

Simon: Oooh, is that a bit of a blush I see on your cheeks?

Aaron: **No! My face always goes red when I'm thinking.**

Simon: OK. So have you thought yet?

Aaron: **I guess it's Emily Windsnap.**

Simon: I thought so! What's so special about Emily?

Aaron: **I don't know. I just like being with her. When we're together, I feel different about myself and about everything that's happened to me. I feel happier than I've felt for a long time, put it that way.**

Simon: Aww, that's lovely. OK, next question – what was the best day of your life?

Aaron: **The day the curse was lifted from my family.**

Simon: What do you want to be when you grow up?

Aaron: I think I'd like to be an explorer. I'd love to travel the world – maybe even swim all the way around it!

Simon: And finally, Aaron, how do you feel about going to Allpoints Island?

Aaron: SO excited. Halflight Castle already feels like my old life. I just can't wait to get started on my new one.

Simon: Well, Aaron, thank you so much for joining us and being so candid about yourself. I wish you all the very best in your new life!

Aaron: Thank you.

Don't miss Emily Windsnap's
next exciting adventure

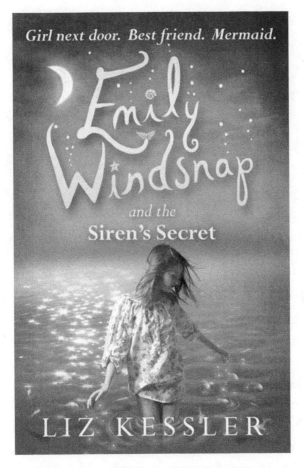

Read on for a special preview
of the first chapter

Prologue

*I*t wasn't a night for going out. Not unless you had to.

Sharp tunnels of wind whistled and shrieked around every corner. Trees bowed and shook and broke. Rain splattered viciously down at the pavements.

Out at sea, it was even worse. On the water, the storm had turned swells into walls the size of tower blocks. Waves foamed hungrily, like giant rabid dogs.

Anyone who knew about the sea knew this

meant one thing: Neptune was angry.

And anyone wild or crazy or brave enough to be out on such a night might have seen two figures in the distance, way out at sea, way beyond safe. A man leaned out from his fishing boat, calling to a woman in the water below him. 'Take it. Take it. Keep it close.'

'What is it?' the woman called back, shouting to be heard over the thunderous waves.

The man shook his head. 'I can't hear you!' Leaning further out, he added, 'When it's safe again, find me.'

'How?' she called, panic hitting her as hard as the waves that were now dragging them further and further apart.

He pointed to the parcel he had just given her. 'The shell!' she thought she heard him say, and then he added something that sounded like, 'There's magic in it.'

The woman thought about what she was leaving and the pain of it slapped against her harder than the next wave. 'What about –'

The wave washed the rest of her question away – but he knew what she was asking.

'I'll look after everything,' he called. 'Everything. Don't worry. It will be OK. Go now. Go, before it's too late.'

A moment later, the onlooker would have seen them part, each disappearing behind the hills and mountains of the raging sea. Then they would have wondered if they'd imagined the whole thing, because surely no one would go out on a night like this.

Not unless they had to.

Chapter One

I know you're going to think I'm crazy when I say this, but something about my life wasn't right.

Why does that make me crazy?

Because for the first time in my life I was living with my mum and dad, together, in our beautiful home at Allpoints Island, with my best friend Shona living just round the corner and my new friend Aaron and his mum living nearby. There was *nothing* wrong with our lives.

Really. Absolutely nothing. No dad to be rescued

from prison; no sea monsters trying to squeeze the life out of me; no storms hurling our home halfway across the planet – all of which *had* happened to me in the last year.

Now all I had was day after day filled with sun, sand, friends, laughter. My life was perfect.

So why had I woken up restless and rattled every morning for the last week? I just didn't get it.

I sat up in bed and stretched, trying to remember what I'd been dreaming about. Fragments from a jumbled mass of weird dreams chased each other round in my head but I couldn't piece them together. All I could remember was the feeling they'd left behind. Not exactly unhappy – but definitely unsettled and, well, not right.

Like I said – crazy. How could anything about my life not be right?

There was something, though, and I couldn't ignore it. What's more, I had the feeling Mum felt the same way. Once or twice, while she was making dinner or reading a book, I'd seen her eyes go all distant and grey, as though she were looking for something far away, something she was missing.

I think deep down inside, I knew what was eating at us both; I knew what we were missing, even before the conversation with Archie that changed everything.

★

'Knock knock, only me!' A familiar voice trilled through the doorway, followed by a familiar thump as Mum's best friend, Millie, landed on the deck.

Fortuna, the boat we lived on, was moored out in the bay, half sunk in the sand so that the lower level was under water. With Dad being a merman, and me being a semi-mer, this meant we could both swim around on the lower level. Mum's bedroom was upstairs, but all the trapdoors in between made it easy for us to live here together. And the long jetty leading out from the beach to the boat was handy for getting on the boat without having to swim – which made it very easy for Millie to visit us without getting more than her feet wet.

She stuck her head round the door. 'Anyone home?'

I dragged myself out of bed and over to the door. Rubbing my eyes, I gestured for her to come in. Not that she needed an invitation. She'd already clambered in through the door and was busily wringing out the bottom of her dress over the side.

'Mum up?' she asked.

I rubbed my eyes and yawned. 'Not yet, I don't think. Why?'

'Someone's coming home!' she said excitedly. 'I just heard it on the seaweed vine.'

'The seaweed vine?'

'Just trying to keep up with the mer-speak,' Millie said, frowning. 'I meant I heard it on the grapevine. Archie's back today!'

That was when I noticed her face. Well, obviously I'd already noticed her face. I was looking straight at it. But I noticed what was on it. Bright blue eyeshadow arching high over each eye, and a thick red line of lipstick smeared across her mouth – and a few teeth. I pointed this out and she peered into the mirror by the door.

'It'sh been nearly tcho weeksh,' she said, wiping lipstick off her teeth with the edge of her sleeve. 'I've misshed him sho much!'

Archie is Millie's boyfriend. He's a merman and he'd been away on an assignment for Neptune.

'Is that Millie?' Mum's voice warbled out from her room. 'Come on in Mill, and stick the kettle on while you're passing.'

I left them to it.

Half an hour later, Mum was dressed and sitting upstairs with Millie in the saloon – that's what you call the living room on a boat. I wanted to go out and play with Shona and Aaron, but Mum said we should all wait with Millie; she was far too excitable to be left on her own.

I waited downstairs with Dad. We had a gymnastics day coming up soon at school and he was helping me with a tricky triple back spin that I had to do as part of the display. I could do two spins

218

perfectly but couldn't manage the third without swallowing a gallon of water.

I was just recovering from my fourth attempt when there was a sharp rap at the door.

'Archie!' I exclaimed.

'I doubt it, little 'un. When did Archie ever knock?'

I laughed. Archie was much more likely to turn up at one of the portholes. Mermen don't usually walk up to the front door.

We both poked our heads up through the trapdoor to see who it was. Mum was answering the door. 'Charles,' she said crisply. 'How nice to see you.'

Mr Beeston. Not exactly our best friend. Well, someone who's spent your entire life lying to you about who you really are, drugging you so you won't remember the truth and spying on you so he can report back to Neptune on your activities doesn't tend to fill your heart with love and warmth, in my experience.

However, after our latest batch of disasters, Neptune had made us all promise to put the past behind us and start afresh. So we'd been trying our best to be friendly and polite ever since.

Mum held the door open for him. 'Why don't you join us?' she said. 'We're just having a cup of tea.'

'Well I, I mean, I don't want to, you know,

I wouldn't like to be in your way,' he stammered, but came in anyway and sat down on the little sofa in the middle of the saloon.

'Hello, Emily,' he said, nodding at me and flattening his hair down.

'Hi,' I said and turned to swim back down, but Dad gave me a nudge.

'Go on up, now; you need to be polite, remember,' he said under his breath.

With a sigh, I pulled myself up through the trapdoor. As I did, I felt the familiar tingling feeling in my tail. Sitting on the side, I watched it flap and wave in the water. The tingling grew stronger, the purply green shimmer faded, my tail stiffened – and then it melted away and my legs emerged. I rubbed the tingle away. It always gave me pins and needles changing back from being a mermaid and my legs were wobbly for a moment, so I didn't stand up straight away.

'I believe Archieval is due back today,' Mr Beeston was saying to Mum as I dangled my legs over the trapdoor. He'd obviously been listening to the grapevine, too. That didn't surprise me. He always seemed to find out what was going on. Probably had spies working for him all over the place.

I knew we were meant to be friends now, but I still didn't trust him and I didn't see how Mum and Dad could be so happy to forgive and forget.

'So I've heard,' Mum said. Millie had got up to check herself out in the mirror again. She pulled at her hair and straightened her dress and was getting her lipstick out of her bag again when there was a noise downstairs.

'That's him!' Millie squeaked. 'He's back!'

We all raced over to the trapdoor and looked down. Sure enough, two seconds later Archie appeared in the large porthole that we use as the downstairs door. He looked up. Grinning broadly, he flicked his dark hair off his face and swam across to the trapdoor. 'Hello all,' he said, looking straight at Millie.

Mum laughed. 'Right, come on, let's get a cup of tea and leave the lovebirds to it,' she said.

Mr Beeston gave Archie a quick nod. 'Good to see you back, Archieval,' he said before following Mum into the kitchen.

'Mine's an Earl Grey,' Millie called over her shoulder, without taking her eyes off Archie for a second.

'So let me get this straight,' Dad said as we gathered outside. Archie and Dad were in the water next to the boat, the rest of us sitting on the front deck. 'You've been in *Brightport* for the last two weeks?'

Brightport was my home. Well, I should say my

old home. It's where I'd spent all my life up until we moved to Allpoints Island – the only place in the world where humans could officially live alongside merpeople. In other words, the only place in the world where my mum and dad could live together. It's the swishiest place ever, and you couldn't want to live anywhere more perfect – but when my dad said the word 'Brightport' I suddenly got a dull ache in my stomach.

'That's right,' Archie replied. 'I didn't realise that was where the assignment was till we were almost there.'

Mr Beeston nodded seriously. 'Well, you know how important it is to Neptune to keep his assignments top secret. That'show it's always been in *my* experience of working alongside the king,' he said importantly.

Archie ignored him and carried on. 'Cranes and diggers had been spotted at the edge of the town, very close to our merfolk area just off the coast. Shiprock folk were getting scared and Neptune sent us to find out what was going on.'

There it was again, the pain in my stomach, only it was even sharper this time. Shiprock was the merfolk town where Shona used to live. Where I'd first gone to mermaid school. Just the mention of the place was enough to give me a funny twinge; the fact that something might be going wrong there made it twice as bad.

'So what did you find?' Dad asked.

'Most of the activity is on land so we were fairly limited. But we managed to discover that it's Brightport Council who are behind it.'

'What are they doing?' asked Mum.

Archie looked at her. 'Well, that depends who you ask. According to the enormous billboards that you can see from about a mile out at sea, they're "developing unused wasteland". But if you ask any of the merfolk at Shiprock, they're about to bulldoze the whole town to smithereens.'

'What d'you mean?' I asked. 'They can't destroy Shiprock, can they?'

'Depends how far they develop, and how many more cranes and diggers they bring out there. They're dangerously close as it is and their work is causing problems in the sea nearby. There've been daily landslides on the outskirts of Shiprock. Two families have already lost their homes. The whole of Shiprock could collapse if those builders get greedy and try to "develop" further into more of our town.'

'But that's terrible!' I said. I thought of the merpeople I'd seen and met in Shiprock, the school, all the kids, the parents, the old folk.

'It certainly is,' Archie agreed. 'The townsfolk are preparing for disaster as far as they can. Leaders are discussing plans for a major evacuation if needed, but they don't want to cause unnecessary panic. No one knows exactly what Brightport Council have in mind, how far they plan to develop, so it's hard for them to make a plan.'

'Can't Neptune do something?' Mum asked.

'Neptune's put the area on high alert,' Archie replied. 'That means the town will have a unit there at all times, to watch what's going on. Beyond that, there's not much he can do.'

'Not much he can do?' I spluttered. 'We *are* talking about the same Neptune? He's more powerful than anyone!'

'Anyone in the *ocean*,' Archie corrected me. 'On land, he has no power to stop anyone doing anything. All he can do is monitor the situation and decide what kind of response to make, and when to make it.'

'How come you've come back here, then?' Mr Beeston butted in. 'Aren't you deserting your post? If Neptune has decreed that you are needed there at all times –'

'Neptune has decreed that *someone* is needed there at all times,' Archie went on. 'But we need a unit that is capable of getting into more of the area than we can access on our own. I have a few contacts on land, but no one who can really find out what's going on. No one with any influence.'

'So you're not going back?' Millie asked, a slight quiver in her voice.

Archie grinned at her. 'Not yet, I'm not. For one

thing, Neptune prefers me to be at Allpoints Island and keep an eye on things here. And for another – well, we need someone different from me. Someone who can gain access to areas that I can't.' He turned to Mr Beeston. 'Someone like you.'

'Someone like me?' Mr Beeston asked. His face turned crimson as he brushed some invisible dust off his collar. 'Well, of course, with an operation of such importance, Neptune is bound to ask for the most highly skilled, professional team on board, and I have to say, though not greatly surprised, I am flattered and –'

'What I mean is, we need a semi-mer,' Archie said, interrupting Mr Beeston in the middle of what was starting to sound like an acceptance speech for a grand award.

Mr Beeston is like me. Half mer, half person. I didn't know it until a few months ago – but then I didn't know it about myself, either, until I went swimming with school for the first time.

'We need someone who has access to the human world as well as the mer world,' Archie went on.

Mr Beeston sniffed and examined his collar again. 'So it's not the years of loyalty, highly skilled work and dedicated training that you're after? It's the fact that I've got legs,' he said.

'And a tail,' I put in. He gave me a look of scorn.

Archie reached into the bag slung by his side and pulled something out. 'Look, it's not just that,' he said. 'You're wanted there.' He passed a bundle of papers on to the deck.

Mr Beeston picked it up. 'What's this?'

'One of my fisherman contacts smuggled it out to me,' Archie said. 'Read it.'

Mr Beeston unfolded the papers. 'It's just a list of names,' he said.

'Read the sentence at the top.'

Mr Beeston cleared his throat. 'We, the undersigned, believe important jobs should be operated by people, not computers. Don't let hi-tech development get out of hand. Reinstate the lighthouse keeper! Bring back Mr Beeston!'

Mr Beeston flicked through the pages of names. 'Well, I —' he began. 'I mean, I —' He looked up at Archie. 'This isn't a joke?'

Archie shook his head.

'The people of the town want me back?'

Archie nodded.

'And Neptune needs me?'

'He does.'

Mr Beeston pulled himself up straighter and higher. 'Well, then,' he said. 'I cannot let them down. I must return to Brightport.'

Which was the exact moment I realised why I'd been having bad dreams every night and waking up sad every morning — and why my insides had ached at the mention of Brightport.

I was homesick. It was as simple as that.

226

Mum turned to Dad. 'Jake,' she said. 'I – I –'

Dad swam over to the side and reached up to take her hand. I looked at Mum's face and I recognised the look in her eyes. It was saying the same thing as mine. It had been saying the same thing all along. These last few weeks when I'd caught her staring into the distance – I suddenly realised what it was she was searching for, what she was missing.

'She wants to go home,' I said.

Dad glanced at me. 'We are home, little 'un,' he said with a quick laugh. Then he turned to Mum. 'Aren'twe?'

Before she could answer, Archie broke in. 'There's something else,' he said. 'I didn't know how to ask, but maybe this is a good time.'

Dad turned to him. 'What is it?'

'Neptune wants a team. If there's going to be trouble, he needs more than just one of us there. Beeston is a good choice for keeping Shiprock under control, and his contacts make him ideal for getting information on the Brightport side of things, especially using the lighthouse keeper cover again.'

Mr Beeston shuffled and flattened his hair down. Before he could launch into another Oscars acceptance speech, Archie added, 'I put your name forward as his assistant.'

'Me?' Dad asked. 'Neptune would put *me* in a

position of responsibility, after – well, after where I've been?'

Dad's not a criminal or anything, but he was sent to prison for marrying my mum. Intermarriage between merpeople and humans used to be highly illegal. But not any more. In fact, Neptune had now decided he wanted to bridge the gap between humans and merpeople – and he'd decided we were the ones to help him.

He'd told us we had to bring the two worlds together, get humans and merpeople to live in peace. And that was another thing: how could we change the world so that humans and merpeople lived in peace together if we were living out here in the one bit of the world where they already did? Everything was pointing to the same conclusion: we had to go back to Brightport.

Archie was still talking to Dad. 'Neptune doesn't hold on to the past,' he was saying. 'He knows you are loyal and dependable.'

'And married to a human,' Dad said.

'Exactly. That's the whole point. One of you to find out more about what's going on with the Brightport folk and one of you keeping an eye on things in Shiprock. Between you two and Beeston, we might just be able to avert a major disaster for the entire town.'

'You're not asking me to spy on my old friends, are you?' Mum asked.

'Not at all! Beeston and Jake will do most of the work. Just keep your eyes and ears open, in case you hear anything that the others miss; anything that could be a problem for the mer community at Shiprock. If anyone else needs to be rehoused, we'd rather they know in advance, so they can get all their belongings and move of their own accord, rather than wake up one morning to a bulldozer in their front cave.'

'Do you think that could really happen?' Mum asked.

'Absolutely. And I'll tell you something else: if another house is destroyed, folk there will *really* start to panic. Neptune doesn't like being in a position like this, where he has no control over what's going on. He's not used to it. If these plans cause more problems, he might decide to exhibit his power by ordering a full-scale evacuation – and most folk are *desperate* to avoid that.'

Dad looked up at Mum. 'What do you think?'

Mum chewed slowly on a thumb nail. 'I think we've been told to find ways to bring the human and the mer worlds together,' she said. 'If the human world is doing something that could threaten merpeople, then it's our duty to stop that from happening.'

Dad reached up and took her hand. 'I agree,' he said. 'This could be our first chance to start putting into practice the instructions that Neptune gave us.'

'Exactly. That's what Neptune said, too.'

Dad looked at Archie. 'What do you mean? What did he say?'

'That it was time you got on with your task. He said to tell you this was an opportunity to prove to him that he picked the right family for the job. He said it would be your first test.'

Dad puffed his chest out and nodded firmly. 'That's decided it, then,' he said. 'We don't have a choice.'

I felt a bubble of excitement rise through my body, tickling my insides and snaking up through my throat. 'We're going back to Brightport?' I asked, holding my breath while I waited for their answer.

Mum and Dad looked at each other and nodded. Then Mum turned to me. 'Yes, darling,' she said, with the first smile I'd seen on her face in days. 'We're going home.'